NEVER THE TWAIN

TE HODDEN

EIGHT YEARS AGO, LAST CHRISTMAS

TANNER'S KISS GOODBYE

It shouldn't have been a kiss goodbye. It was too perfect.

The moment California Gregory joined me under my umbrella, thunder rumbled through the station, and the rain went from a light pattering of a snare drum beat, to the crashing percussion of a military tattoo, sweeping across the platforms, and hammering on the canopy. It blotted out the railway, and reduced the city beyond to a blur of neon lights.

Callie gripped me tight, squeezing me in an embrace. "Hey."

"Hey," I said, with more confidence than I felt.

People said Callie had green eyes, but that fell far short of their beauty. She had eyes all the colours of the ocean, they were grey, green, blue and brown, all swirled together in whirlpools that went on forever, down into the darkness of her pupils, and just happened to give the overall impression of a startling green. They said she had a pretty smile, but that was wrong. She had countless smiles, for any possible occasion. She had smiles that were warm and homely, rosy and loving, soft and sad, or thin dangerously angry smiles.

Callie was about my own age, in her mid-twenties, beautiful in a curvy, cuddly, very full figured kind of way. It was real beauty, the kind that didn't care about dress sizes.

That last time I saw her, her eyes were full of hopes and regrets, her smile raw, and vulnerable. Her trembling fingers curled around mine, as her heart hammered so hard I could feel it against my chest.

I'd rehearsed all the things I was meant to say, a thousand times over. I'd played them through my head, endlessly, and now... now they stuck in my craw.

"You were wrong," I said. "What you said to me was wrong. I never... faked friendship with you. I never pretended. Whatever else I felt, whatever I hoped for, and longed for, was grown from our friendship. I loved you long, long, long before I fell in love with you. And... and... if that love was pathetic, if it was soft, and stupid, and puppy dog kindness, then… so what? I'm not a billionaire. I don't ride a motorcycle, or get in fights, and I don't Christmas in Italy. I don't even know the difference between Christmasing somewhere, and just being there for Christmas." I looked at her. "The things I do? The ones I think I'm good at? Being there when you need a lift, or a loan, or not to be alone? I… didn't do those because I fancied you. I did those because we were friends, and they were right. Even after I fell for you, that's all I tried to be, because it's all I dared to believe you might want from me. It's all I ever thought you would see in me. We said before we started this, that if it didn't work out, we would still be friends." I drew a breath. "You can dump me, you can say that stuff about me, you can… pretend that everything we had these last few weeks didn't count, but I am begging you… please don't believe everything we were is gone. Please don't believe the friendship doesn't count. And you best not pretend it ends this easily."

Callie squeezed the hug. "Oh Christ. You thought I

meant…any of that?"

"You were very loud," I said, "and seemed very sure."

She shook her head, and cupped my cheek. "Feel free to hate me for that."

There was a rumble, as a train slowed into the station.

I cleared my throat, and took the present from my satchel. It was bubble-wrapped rather than gift wrapped. "This is me proving I'm still your friend."

"I believe you," she said. "Give it to me after Christmas, and that way…"

"It's an Action Dan Annual from the year Adam was born," I said. "It's pristine. No dog ears, no creases, the puzzles untouched, and the 3D glasses haven't even been popped out the perforated page."

Callie gasped. "No… You can't get these. Adam has been after this for…" She frowned at me, her nose wrinkling. "Why are you doing this?"

"Because I love you enough to want you to be happy, and if… that's with Adam, I want to help you." I looked at my feet. "Because… it's what a less selfish friend would have done to begin with."

Callie's smile changed. Something about the way she leaned warned me to close my eyes, to welcome the kiss.

It was the kind of kiss that slowed time, that made raindrops hang in the air, and let the rest of the world fade into shadows and silence. She was gently hungry, caressing my lips with her, drinking my soul away.

We broke for air rosy and giggling.

"What…" I flustered. "What was that?"

Callie chewed her lip. "That was me saying goodbye to my least-worst boyfriend. When I get home in January, I'll be saying hello to my best friend again, right?"

"Movie nights on Friday?" I offered.

She grinned. "Absolutely."

I stooped for her case, and escorted her to the doors of the train. She dropped her case on the luggage rack, and nodded to where she was taking a seat. I followed outside, smiling at her all the way. She sat down and put her hand to the window. I placed mine over hers.

The warning tone beeped as the doors closed.

I stepped back, and watched her as the train rumbled away.

*

I juggled pans across the heat, making sure two orders of chicken, and one of duck were going to reach the plate at the same time. "How are we doing on that burger Squeak?"

"Thirty seconds from the plate," the burly hefty man behind me reported.

I dropped the plates and started assembling my dishes, with a delicate hand and an eye for detail, cleaning around the plating marks with a cloth, before I added a sweep of sauce and a pretty little garnish. My plates reached the counter the same time as Squeak's. I spiked the ticket and slapped the bell. One of the waitresses galloped over to grab the plates, and danced into the crowd with them.

Fred, my big sister (who must never be called Francesca), stared at me over the tasting plate she was assembling. "What the bloody Hell have you done?"

"I met her," I said, "at the station before she made it to the airport."

"Did you try to win her back?" Fred demanded. "I swear to God…"

"No." I held up my hands. "I made it right. I reminded her we were meant to stay friends if it went wrong and I…"

"No!" Squeak said. "Wrong thing to do!"

"What?" I asked. "You are still friends with both your ex-wives!"

Squeak shrugged. "No. I tolerate my ex-wives and can't avoid them. I do not go looking to kick that hornet's nest."

"What," Fred said, slowly, "did you do?" Her eyes widened. "You found the book! You idiot! You threw her back into the Adam Twydal whirlwind."

"I helped her fix things with her one true," I said.

"Oh good." Squeak grinned. "You can clear up the mess when he sends her crashing back to Earth again. Did you invite her back to movie night?”

“She’s still a friend,” I said. “Of course she is welcome to movie night.”

“With Adam?” Squeak asked.

“I…” I flustered. “Yeah, I suppose. If he wanted…”

Fred rubbed the bridge of her nose. “Do you know what you have done there, Tanner? You have doomed yourself to a friendship, without benefits, with a double side order of blame, resentment, and drama.”

“Wait…” Squeak spluttered. “Isn’t that marriage?”

I shrank away. “I wanted her to be happy.”

Fred sighed, and hugged me. “I know. Of course, you did. But… you just ruined movie night! You just doomed us to Adam ‘has all the opinions and no inner monologue’ Twydal, at movie night!”

“Right,” I snatched a ticket from the rack.

“This conversation,” Squeak said, “is not over.”

“One Duck, One Steak rare, one side salad, one polenta chips,” I said.

"Chef!" The others replied, as we set to our stations.

*

Fred and I walked home along the seafront, on the wide concrete path between the sea wall and the pebble beaches pinned together by groynes.

"So, are you going to tell me about this middle manager you met at the club?" I asked.

Fred sighed. "If they actually ring me back, I'll let you know."

"Oh come on," I said, an arm around her hips. "You could at least tell me her name."

Fred smiled. "I will, when I am sure there is something to tell."

I paused a moment. "Did I really do the wrong thing with Callie?"

Fred stopped smiling. She took one of her 'we need to talk' breaths. "You did the kind thing, and the noble thing, but it wasn't the smart thing. If I were her, I would be looking to move out the house as soon as I can, because…

there is a reason everybody tells you they want to stay your friend, and nobody means it. It is really, really, really hard not to hate seeing them happier with somebody than they were with you. It's even harder seeing every little thing you would not have done to hurt them. It's a fool's errand."

I nodded.

"Especially," she whispered, "when you are still crazy for each other."

"I told you," I said, "we are now just…"

"I know what you said," Fred laughed. "I know how much you are making a point of not saying."

We reached her terrace, and she jumped up onto the sea wall.

Fred smiled at me. "Tanner…" Her tone firmed up. "What you did today? That would have been one of Mum's stories. She would have been churning that out over every single glass of wine."

I smiled. "You think?"

She nodded. "We'll work all of this out. I promise."

I headed on my way, following the sea wall a while longer, then cutting up a passageway into the streets. I almost made it home, I was about to cross the road, to the blunt faced, mid terrace Victorian townhouse that I had grown up in. The ground floor and cellar was mine. I rented out three more flats on the other two floors, the smallest of which was Callie's.

I felt the sound rather than heard it.

A high pitched whistle, like a kettle too long on the boil, that filled my skull. It set my jaw, and make my bones grind together. I froze, unable to make my leaden feet take another step. The amber streetlights were suddenly painfully bright.

Callie was floating in the middle of the road. She hovered about two meters over the street, floating like she was under water, air bubbling from her lips, her hair spread out like a halo, her long winter coat billowing about her.

I gasped for breath.

She reached out for me, her eyes full of fear, her body

twitching and squirming. Then, suddenly, she was still. Her eyes out of focus, her chest unmoving, and her breath stopped.

"No!" I clawed at my head. "No! What is…"

A roar of engines and a sweep of lights snapped me back to reality. I turned, seeing too late the boy racer who had tried to take the corner too fast, hitting the kerb and grinding against the wall. I didn't have time to move, or anywhere to go.

The headlights swallowed me, and tidal wave of pain crashed over me, and I bounced off the windscreen and into the road.

I lay on the black-top, gasping for breath, drowning in pain, as the world went fuzzy. The car sped away, the lights fading into the distance, leaving the darkness to swallow me.

Callie's Last Kiss

Eight years ago, I stood in the rain, to hide my tears.

Just keep in mind this is the story of Our Last Kiss, which is kind of my redeeming moment, but… before we get there I have to make a few mistakes first, and… this is not going to be pretty.

If you want to hate me, now is a good place to start.

For what it's worth, I had just made one of the hardest decisions of my life, and I have spent far more of the years since wondering if it was the right choice, than I would care to admit.

At the time it seemed simple. I'd had a several years with Adam, who was, for all his faults, everything a girl should have wanted. He was handsome, he was exciting, he was dangerous (and yes, that time he beat up a guy for harassing me in a club was so incredibly hot it burned at my common sense) and he was rich. He was never less than perfectly dressed and impeccably groomed, and he was so far rooted in my heart and soul, that when people told me I was the one who had blown it, and let him walk off, I had half believed them.

I wanted to believe them.

I was nineteen when I met Adam, he was twenty six. We fell in love quick, fell out of love a week later, made up, managed a year, before we had two months apart, and then stuck it until I was twenty five, and almost through University.

An heir to billions has certain advantages as a boyfriend. I travelled around, and didn't have to worry about affording my education, or moving to the UK, and living in London, until…

Until her sent a text message to the wrong number and I found out why he had been visiting

Paris so much without me.

Long story short, I moved out, and couldn't afford anywhere in London. I ended up commuting from the coast, on the High Speed train every day. My new landlord, Tanner, was a chef, who lived downstairs, who... over that year became a friend, then a good friend, then... Then one day there were a thousand little kindnesses. He drove me to college when the trains were cancelled. He cooked for me when I was too exhausted to fend for myself. He left me wriggle room on rent, and helped me look for a job, and... when I was more alone than anybody should ever be, he held me, and he listened to me talk, and he looked at me.

Oh, I knew how he felt about me, long before that. I knew he wouldn't have taken advantage of me. He wasn't going to kiss me, or ask a date, or strike while I was vulnerable. If he was that kind of guy, I wouldn't have wanted him. I wouldn't have longed for the safety of his company, for the little fairy-light glow in my heart I got knowing that no matter how bad my day, he would have food, wine, and the world's most comfortable shoulder.

There came a point that was all I wanted, and so… one night when I really needed good food and a long hug, I kissed him.

For a little while, I teetered on the edge of happiness. Most of me wanted to let go and fall. I couldn't imagine myself being anywhere, or more content, than with Tanner. I only went to my flat to collect mail. I lived in his flat, slept in his bed, wrote my thesis on his sofa, and wondered if we could rent all the flats, and afford a nice little place of our own. Somewhere with room for kittens, and a kids. Somewhere I could home too when I worked out what to do with my degree.

But, there was one traitorous splinter of my heart that would always dream of excitement, and luxury, and miss the feel of Adam's lips on the back of my neck, as he put his arms around me, and rubbed against me, driving every one of my nerves wild in a way nobody else ever had, or would.

I couldn't live with that bit of him in my heart. I had to be rid of it. I needed… closure. So… I messaged Adam, and told him we should meet. We should talk. We hadn't left on good terms, we both had somebody new, we had both moved on, and I had every intention of never being hurt by him, or anybody like him, ever again.

It… didn't work out that way.

I met him on in a café and slapped him so hard the whole place held its breath. He nodded, gave me a sorry smile, and kissed me. Or I kissed him. It happened so fast, it was difficult to tell.

That splinter in my heart burned so bright it set light to everything else. Everything burned away from me, and I was lost to my instincts. They carried me to his hotel room, to the honeymoon suite (of course). I was weightless. My heart ran so hot, and so fast, I floated into bed at him, ripping and clawing at his clothes, hungry for the taste of his sweat as I muffled my screams on his shoulder.

I was… home. I was back where I belonged, writhing on his bed in a category ten orgasm, thinking I never wanted to be anywhere else, feeling anything else, wanting anything else.

We lay in a sweaty tangle after, and watched the night sky with the lights out, talking through, making amends, coming to an understanding that felt right.

And then my phone rang, and Tanner's face smiled out of the screen.

"Who's that?" Adam asked.

My heart shrivelled and died in my chest. "He's kind of my boyfriend."

"Kind of?" Adam smiled. "That sounds

serious."

"It is." I realised what I just said. "Until a few hours ago, it was. I…"

"You never gave up on me, so easily," he said, laying back. "I'm just saying."

"Hey…" I warned him. "Don't do this."

"What?" He flicked through my phone at the pictures. "You have a lot more pictures of me, than him. And… let's be honest. Look at him. The night a guy who looks like that, took a girl who looks like you home, the world went out of balance."

"It isn't like that," I said. "With you everything is like being tossed into a hurricane and losing control. We run on passions and fury, and… animal instincts. Tanner is like… the feeling I get when I wear the sweater your mom knitted for me. It's cosy, and warm, and all about the memories. It's safe, and gentle, and… we curl on the sofa to watch movies, he makes grilled cheese for me, and…"

"Grilled cheese?" Adam stroked my cheek, and raised an eyebrow. "How can I compete with grilled cheese?"

Okay, here's the secret to how Adam gets to you. It's in the smile he wore as he stroked my cheek. It's the devil's smile. It convinces you that whatever he's saying is okay, because it's a joke. It makes you smile back, because you're having a secret joke, just between you two, and the rest of the world can be damned. No matter how much you are going to regret it later.

I smiled. I laughed. "He's okay. Don't be mean."

"He stole my girl," Adam said. "He sounds a dick."

Somewhere, a couple of my braincells fell back into place. Too few, too late, but enough for a few thoughts to make it through the afterglow of that cat ten orgasm. "No. Don't do that. He isn't."

Adam gave me a guilty smile. "Okay. Was it a good grilled cheese?"

"It was just before we started seeing each other. I was homesick," I said quietly, "and lonely, and you had just sent me a text meant for somebody else, and…"

I ran out of words. I couldn't tell him how much that text message hurt. How much it made me hate myself for everything I should have hated him for. I couldn't begin to tell him how far I fell that night, or how much it meant to land in Tanner's arms. He didn't understand, and I couldn't tell him, so he just held me, and gave me tea, and promised not to leave until I was okay. Then he made me a grilled cheese that tasted just like one from my favourite food truck. Weeks before I had mentioned, in passing, that cheese on toast didn't cut it, and that even my mom hadn't made a sandwich like this one diner I used to love.

Tanner fried the bread just right, and had different kinds of cheese with bechamel sauce, and he grilled it until there was just enough golden brown crunch.

"What happens now?" I asked.

Adam took my hand. "I'm going to do better." He meant it. I could see it in his eyes. There was something in his eyes. His armour of ego, swagger, and jokes had been stripped away. His eyes were wounds down to his soul. "I'm clean. I'm sober. I've… I've seen how I hurt people, how I hurt you, and… I need to make it right. Not just with you, but… especially with you."

"I've been happy," I said. "I've been so happy."

"So why are you here?" He demanded. "What did we just do?"

I shook my head. "I can't… I didn't…"

Adam sighed. "This can be goodbye, but… be

honest to Grilled Cheese. He… sounds like he did okay by you. Don't lie. It'll hurt him."

"Voice of experience?" I asked.

He nodded. "The worst."

*

Okay, just a heads up: If you don't hate me by now, you really need to start.

I'm not going to tell you everything that happened when I finally told Tanner. You don't need a blow by blow account, and if I'm honest, I don't remember what was said. I mean… I remember the subjects covered, but not the words.

I've been breaking up since I was thirteen. I've gotten pretty good at it, and on a good day, I can win the argument with a brutal efficiency. Go in hard and fast at the first bell, and put the other guy in the corner before they can land a strike that hurts you. After some years with Adam, I was a goddamned heavyweight.

I don't think Tanner had... had a real girlfriend before. He'd dated, but it had never stuck, and he was a virgin. Let's assume he hadn't, because, he sure as Hell hadn't broken up before.

By the time I realised he wasn't going to fight me, I was smashing him over the face with a metaphorical chair, spilling his teeth over the proverbial mat.

It got away from me. I can blame it on the guilt, on the pain of knowing I had betrayed him, on needing to believe it was his fault not mine, so I didn't have to look at what I had done too closely. So I didn't have to say words like 'unfaithful' or 'liar'.

By the time I caught up with myself, I had stepped well past anything remotely reasonable, calling him dull, or a bad fit, cloying and suffocating, and was hitting him with left-jab questions. Was he ever my friend, or just horny?

Did he mean any of his little kindnesses, or was that him gaslighting me? Did he know really think I would ever truly love him?

Somehow… his not fighting me made me angrier. It made me scream until my throat was raw.

I stopped short of calling him pathetic.

I opened my mouth, but I couldn't say it. I heard Adam's voice screaming those words at me, the first time we broke up.

The memory stole my fight from me.

I caught my breath. "I'm going away for Christmas. I'll try and find a new place to live when I'm back for the new term. I'll…"

I don't know if he even heard me. I could see him shaking. His expression was one of hurt, not rage, but his eyes were cold, and his fingers had curled into fists.

There were nine days between the fight, and my going to Venice. Adam was already there, but I had work to get finished at University. I should have got a hotel in London, and cut us off, but I kept thinking every night, I would find a way to make our peace, to set it right, to explain.

And every night I was too scared to try.

I would see him slouching home from his restaurant and I would remember how I felt after all those breakups. It would crush my heart.

I did see everybody for Movie Night on Friday. I mean, that was non-negotiable. Even Adam made it, dropping in to the restaurant, for one night, to cuddle me in one of the booths, sip beer, and watch a crummy old English horror movie. I don't think he quite got on the right frequency for the evening. He challenged every joke, like it was a serious debate, and went looking for ways to lock horns with Tanner.

Tanner, for his part, went above and beyond in terms of being polite and gracious, even when

Adam made a few barbed comments about the food. "So, you didn't train in France then?" Or something. (Adam was joking. Later that night he would describe the meatball subs as, and I quote "so good they made me tingle somewhere food isn't meant to touch.")

The one time I got to be alone with Tanner all he asked was if I was okay, and reminded me that if I ever needed to talk, he was still there. I smiled, and nodded, and patted his cheek.

Eventually, I packed for Christmas, and went to get the train to London, so I could get a connection to the airport, and… maybe in Venice, with the strength of Adam's support (oh boy was he good at making you feel strong, indestructible even) I could find the right way to say it.

Maybe, but I didn't believe it.

I stood in the rain to hide my tears, refusing to let the world see I was pathetic.

There are not the words to tell you how it felt to see Tanner running down onto the platform to find me. A heartbeat of terror, that stole my breath and made my knees buckle, instantly forgotten when I saw his smile. That smile. The one he had the night he gave me grilled cheese.

I stared at him, wishing I knew what to say. Nothing sprang to mind, so I grabbed him. He put his hands on my side in one of his 'I'm here' touches, the ones that promised I would never be alone, and gave me one of those 'I'm scared too, but everything will be okay, because we're doing this together' looks.

He could say a lot with a look. He had a 'I don't know how to tell you how beautiful you are, but you can see it in my eyes,' look, and a 'you are terrified you just wrote several hundred words of crap, but you are doing so great.' My favourite was his 'don't ever stop holding me' look.

"Hey," he said, endearingly terrified. "You were wrong. What you said to me was wrong. I never… faked friendship with you. I never pretended. Whatever else I felt, whatever I hoped for, and longed for, was grown from our friendship. I loved you long, long, long before I fell in love with you. And… and… if that love was pathetic, if it was soft, and stupid, and puppy dog kindness, then… so what? I'm not a billionaire. I don't ride a motorcycle, or get in fights, and I don't Christmas in Italy. I don't even know the difference between Christmasing somewhere, and just being there for Christmas. The things I do? The ones I think I'm good at? Being there when you need a lift, or a loan, or not to be alone? I… didn't do those because I fancied you. I did those because we were friends, and they were right. Even after I fell for you, that's all I tried to be, because it's all I dared to believe you might want from me. It's all I ever thought you would see in me. We said before we started this, that if it didn't work out, we would still be friends." He stopped for breath before he turned purple. "You can dump me, you can say that stuff about me, you can… pretend that everything we had these last few weeks didn't count, but I am begging you… please don't believe everything we were is gone. Please don't believe the friendship doesn't count. And you best not pretend it ends this easily."

So many of my fears crumbled to dust as he spoke. I mean, I had hurt him, maybe deeper and harder than I had thought, but… in ways I could put right. Damage control was possible. Things were pretty burned, but this could be okay. Like a forest growing back after a fire, or… broken bones growing back stronger.

I could save this friendship.

In that moment, in his arms, with all that

weight off my shoulders, that seemed as important as making things right with Adam had been.

"Oh Christ," I said, trying to disguise my relief as a laugh. "You thought I meant… any of that?"

The poor guy squirmed. "You were very loud," he said, quivering, "and seemed very sure."

Ain't that the truth? "Feel free to hate me for that."

He wrestled himself into something close to composed as the train rumbled into the station. "This is me proving I'm still your friend."

"I believe you," I promised. "Give it to me after Christmas, and that way…"

"It's an Action Dan Annual from the year Adam was born," He blurted in a hurry. "It's pristine. No dog ears, no creases, the puzzles untouched, and the 3D glasses haven't even been popped out the perforated page."

That couldn't be. I mean… How?

I shook my head. "No… You can't get these. Adam has been after this for…Why are you doing this?"

He turned scarlet. "Because I love you enough to want you to be happy, and if… that's with Adam, I want to help you. Because… it's what a less selfish friend would have done to begin with."

I suddenly knew what I needed to do, for my sake more than his. I needed to put a full stop to my feelings. Everything changed with our first kiss, and everything was going to change again with the last.

One perfect kiss, saying goodbye to what could have been, and hello to all we were going to be from now on.

I closed my eyes, and fell into the kiss, feeling us both submerge down into that darkness where there is nothing else in the world beyond our fingertips, where the whole world was in the lightning storm of sensation where our lips met. His shock was cute, his hunger was exciting, but it was the tender longing that I'm always going to remember. Once he knew what he was doing, let his shields down, and offered himself to me in return.

We broke for air rosy and giggling.

"What…" Tanner looked horrified, like thought that was goodbye. "What was that?"

I pinched my lip with my teeth. "That was me saying goodbye to my least-worst boyfriend. When I get home in January, I'll be saying hello to my best friend again, right?"

"Movie nights on Friday?" He offered.

"Absolutely!" I assured him.

And that was all either of us needed to be sure.

*

I know you don't have any reason to believe I

ever intended to make good on those promises, but I did. I needed to. I needed friends who were my friends. I was going back to Adam an older, wiser woman than the girl who marched out on him. I was stronger, and my friends, friends as close as family, were one of my strengths.

If I was going back to Adam's world, I needed to take some of my world with me. I needed clothes in my drawer that he didn't send a stylist to choose for me, and books on the shelf from charity shops. I needed movie nights at the restaurant, and friends I could fart in front of.

I needed friends who could see me when I was uncaged from my bra, and free from the blistering Hell of high heels, when I was in pyjamas, and when I needed to complain about boob sweat and a bad back.

I needed my little flat on the coast to still feel like home.

*

"So," I asked, "where are we staying?"

Adam didn't answer. He stowed my bag in the motorboat, and cast us off.

"Adam?" I looked up at the buildings that loomed over us. Venice had a certain ageless beauty, a pleasantly haunted sensation that saturated the dark stone buildings, with their shadowy nooks and echo filled passageways. I was already imagining a banquet hall to dine in, a ballroom to dance in, and a roaring fire by which we could snuggle, and talk, or… lose ourselves in each other for a while.

We sped out of the canals and into the wider, more open waters of the lagoon, past the crowded marinas.

"You bought a yacht," I said, with a chuckle.

"I was single, and needed something to impress the socialites."

"Is that why you have the speed boat?" I asked.

"I was thinking of taking up racing," he said, flashing me a smile.

"Adam… No…" I stared at him. "I'm exhausted, and I just want…"

He gunned the engine. We skipped on a wave, as we flew forwards. "Pardon?"

I had to shout over the gale-force wind as we shot through the water. "Isn't this a little dangerous?"

"It's why you have to hold on tight!"

"Can I have a life jacket?" I demanded.

"Oh please!" He looked at me with a playful frown. "Don't you trust me?"

Fate answered him with a sudden crunch as we hit something beneath the water, that scored against the keel of the boat with a banshee howl, and sent it rolling onto its side.

In movies it all would have happened in slow motion, as the water came up to swallow me, and the world rolled with the boat. It would have had the momentum of a glacier, slow, but unstoppable, letting you notice every horrifying detail.

Life wasn't like that.

It happened in a blink of an eye, there was the deafening growl of impact, a confusion of lurching motion, and the ice cold waves that felt like a concrete wall falling on me.

I plunged into the darkness, the cold stealing my breath, the pain and shock stealing my thoughts. For a few moments, I survived only on instinct, fighting and clawing my way for the surface, as the cold crushed my chest. My lungs burned, not just to draw in air, but with the charcoal heat of the bad air trapped inside. I could feel it scalding my lungs like acid. I kicked in the direction I hoped was up, I struggled to the lights I hoped were the surface.

My heartbeat deafened me, blotting out all else.

My burning lungs heaved, spewing bubbles of fetid air.

Cold water choked in my gullet, and strangled me, my vision fading to darkness.

*

A sound woke me with a start.

I was in a hospital bed, wearing nothing but a surgical robe, tied to a bed by the oxygen mask over my mouth and nose, feeding me air, and the web of pipes and cables that tethered me to machines. Adam was kneeling by my bed, asleep, his head on my side, an arm across my belly.

The sound was a steam whistle, the kind you used to see in old movies, calling workers to the factory. It filled my skull, and threatened to shatter my teeth.

I looked to the far side of the room. The city lay beyond my window.

Tanner lay on the floor. Except it wasn't the floor. It was the black-top and white paint of a road. He lay twitching, gasping, his arm bent at an unnatural angle, and a halo of blood growing about his head.

His breathing was… It was the sound of his breathing that would echo in my nightmares. Ragged, wet, burbling breaths, as blood bubbled on his lips.

And then there was silence.

He lay unmoving. His eyes were staring without seeing. His expression sagging, but not peaceful.

He died alone, and scared, impossibly before my eyes.

I screamed.

Adam woke and caught me in a hug. "It's okay.

It's okay. You're safe."

"Tanner. He died, he…"

"No." Adam soothed me. "You hit your head. You're… confused."

I looked to the floor again. Nothing but an easy clean surface. Relief flooded me.

"I think…" I hugged Adam. "I had a nightmare. It was so real."

He held me the way he never would have before. Gentle, safe, welcoming. "It's okay."

The crash, we decided, was nightmare enough.

CALLIE ADRIFT

Oh, how I wish I had understood that message. I wish I had made Adam ring Tanner, or Fred, or the restaurant.

I'm not sure on the timing. Maybe I could have warned them. Tanner wouldn't have believed me, but... her would have waited at the restaurant a while, or taken a taxi, just to be sure I was happy.

Of that, I am sure.

Maybe I was too late. Maybe I would have just gotten to speak to Fred in those final moments and...maybe, just maybe, everything that followed would have been easier.

I didn't.

I learned Tanner was dead when I left hospital and put my phone on. I ignored the dozens of messages at first. I thought they were my friends worrying about me, and I wanted to know what to say before I responded. I wanted to do it right.

Then… I read the messages and it tore my heart to confetti. All my hopes, my dreams, my plans for the perfect balance of my life and Adam's fell to pieces about me.

TANNER ALONE

Callie and Adam were dead.

Fred didn't want to tell me at first. I had been in a medically induced coma for a long time, keeping me back from the cusp of death as I had surgery after surgery, stitching my broken parts back together again. Fred worried it would break me apart again.

When she did tell me, it left me numb and distant.

Fred took my hand. "For a while you were…"

I nodded.

"And…" Fred cleared her throat. "You…"

I looked away. "We… made love."

Fred smiled. "Your first?"

I nodded.

She curled on the bed with me. "She loved you. Maybe just for a little while, but… there were times she was so… so… in love with you."

"And I was with her," I whispered.

Fred nodded. "I'm sorry."

I closed my eyes. "See." I drew a breath. "I wasn't quite so broken as we thought."

"As you thought," Fred mumbled. "You'll find that again. I promise."

I looked at her. "I saw you looking at that nurse."

"So did she. She asked me out." Fred glowed red. "I said yes."

We both grinned, but I don't think either of us felt it.

This Week

CALLIE'S GREY WEEK

The baby faced thirty something, size twenty six, in the dress that nipped and tucked in all the right places to suggest the scaffold of lingerie beneath, thrusting out a pair of breasts like cottage loaves, and squeezing the peachy bottom, was me, California Twydal, and, if I'm honest, I was bored out of my skull.

Today was Wednesday, and the week had yet to find any momentum. It had been bland, grey, and listless. Just like me.

I ambled through the black tie gala, pinching nibbles from trays, and nursing my flute of wine. This should have felt like a homecoming. I was in one of my favourite museums. When I was studying in London I would sit here for hours, staring at some of the Egyptian exhibits, between the bustling of school parties, drinking in the fascinating details of all the little nick-knacks that offered tiny little hints of what ordinary (or not so ordinary) lives had been like all those years ago.

London had not felt like home for a long time. After Tanner died, I tried to still be friends with Fred, and Squeak, but we had drifted apart pretty quickly. She had kept the restaurant going a while, but there had been more money in managing a kitchen for somebody else, and Squeak struck out on his own.

We all went out own way.

I had Adam, and that meant I could go anywhere, and do near enough anything. I became a wife, a home maker, a writer, a patron of the arts and of museums, of charities and foundations.

Those all seemed to involve black tie galas, organised by the same people, with the same string quartets, silent auctions, nibbles and wine. We all wore new dresses, and they all looked the same.

They all felt the same.

They all smelt the same.

It didn't matter if I was at an opera house, gallery, museum, or educational centre. There was a lingering "black tie" scent.

I glanced across the crowded floor. On the far side, of the circular gallery, studying one of the Roman vases in the collection of the new display, was Adam. He had grown broader, heavier, and more rounded these last few years, his beard streaked with silver, and his hair was receding. He was a lot more comfortable in his own skin, and was less inclined to punish it at the gym.

Hey, who was going to complain? He could probably fire them, even if he had to buy the company first.

He smiled back. Tonight, he almost meant it.

Don't get me wrong. He loved me, just as

much as I loved him, but... there was a part of him that was always thinking of some company he was going to buy, take over, or invest in. There was always something that would be the next big thing. If he was considering a new solar panel for the yacht, he would be thinking about solar farms, or tech companies, if he bought a factory and replaced copper wire for an alloy, he could save a few dollars for the same profit and earn another billion.

When we talked about kids, he loved the idea, but there was always something we needed to do first.

When we talked about settling down somewhere, he just wanted to get a few things out the way first.

When we talked about anything, there was always something, and he would need a few months, that became a year, that became... forever.

I stopped talking about kids, about houses, about easing off his grip on the company, and started looking for classes, or charity work, or anything else that would get me out in the world for a little while. I tried a lot of things once.

The problem was we jetted about so often I never got the chance to stick with anything, and there was always going to be another one of these.

Adam raised an eyebrow.

I put a finger on my lips and slipped out of the gala and into one of the side galleries. The one I always used to love. I slipped into my old seat, and sat, watching one of the mummies.

"Hey," I said to the vaguely human bundle of matchwood bones and leathery skin. "Long time no see. How are you doing?"

The mummy stared back.

"Me too," I agreed, resting my chin on my hands. The distant music and laughter echoed through the museum. "Don't tell anybody, okay?"

I took his silence as agreement, and reached up to the locket on my throat, and popped it open. A single small, clear, crystal dropped out into my palm. I placed it on my tongue, and let it melt, in a slightly sweet liquid, and slightly minty fumes that swirled through me.

I lay on the bench, closed my eyes, and waited for the Drift to hit me.

The world turned hazy, and I sunk through the bench.

I dreamt of a night almost like tonight, but with a little more drizzle. I dreamt of Tanner's kitchen, at the restaurant. It was the same old kitchen. The restaurant had been refreshed, twice now, with fresh paint and new furniture. It had gone up in the world. There were new worktops in the kitchen, new equipment (I'd seen the guys use them, and still didn't know what they were for), but it was... the same.

I touched the counter. It was unnaturally cold, like a freezer, but it was solid. I could touch anything, feel it, but not move it. The Dream only allowed me to be an observer, a ghost, not a player in the game.

Tanner was juggling pans, doing something magical with king prawns, chili, lime, mango juice and coriander. Squeak was making burgers, because… well there's always somebody who wants a burger, no matter how posh the restaurant got, and Squeak made fantastic burgers.

Fred was assembling dessert taster plates, with delicate care, but she was a million miles away. She was thinking of her wife. Counting the seconds until they could kiss and talk about the day. I knew the signs. It was in the way she stroked the hair behind her ears. It was in the way she touched the pocket with her wedding ring in.

I walked over to Tanner and put a hand on his shoulder.

He didn't feel me.

Like everything in the dream, he was cold, and felt too…plastic. He was like a rubber doll on a cold day. There was no heat from the hobs, from the flames, from the boiling pots. There was no blast furnace itch on my skin.

The rich aromas though, were perfect. They sizzled in my brain and sent my stomach churning.

Time had not been kind to Tanner. He was weathered and weary, gaunt before his years. His smile had dimmed and faded.

"No luck on the dating app, huh?" I asked, getting as close as I dared.

Tanner didn't answer.

Fred looked up at him. "Hey. So… did you try the App?"

"I…" Tanner rubbed the back of his neck. "I messaged some people."

"And?" Squeak asked.

"One of them saw the video blog," I said.

"Oh!" Fred giggled. "Was she impressed?"

Tanner rolled his eyes. "She told me she loved the meatball recipe, but asked if you were on the app."

Fred rolled her eyes. "That makes sense."

"Yeah," Squeak agreed. "She would want to be sure to block you both…"

They laughed.

I laughed too. I settled on the side, and held onto my little slice of heaven as long as I could.

Somebody stepped into the gallery.

I dragged myself free of the dream, and sat up. Adam leant on a pillar and smiled at me.

"Hey," he whispered. "We could go home, if…"

"I'm okay," I promised. "I just needed a moment."

He nodded. "Mind if I join you?"

I patted the bench, and he joined me, staring at

the mummy.

"Ugly bitch, wasn't she?" He asked.

"I'm not sure I'm go look that good when I'm her age."

He smiled, and draped an arm around me. We settled into an embrace.

Adam tensed. He only did that when he had decided something, and he didn't think I was going to like it. "What if I had to put Paris on hold for a while?"

"You can't even manage a weekend?" I asked.

"There's something in Texas I want to check out. It could be exciting."

"Corporate exciting," I asked, "or real exciting?"

"Hmm." He kissed my cheek. "What are your feelings on controlled-environment farming?"

"Like a big green house?"

He sighed. "I guess you'd rather be in Paris?"

"I would rather be in Paris with my husband," I said. "If I'm going to be alone, I'd rather be in London."

"Sure." Adam nodded, firmly. "Give me a few weeks, and we'll do Paris. I promise."

His smile was warm, but the promise left me feeling all the worst kinds of cold.

*

The next morning was fresh and bright, despite the tinge of frost in the air. Adam had gone before I woke, leaving a note on the bedside table.

Our London apartment was two thirds of the way up one of the space age towers that dominated the London skyline. I sat on the end of the bed, savouring a coffee, watching the sun drag itself out from behind the city, setting the sky on fire.

My dealer answered my text before I was done with the coffee. I dragged myself through a shower, and into some comfortable clothes, and hurried out into the morning.

Cede's current address was a poky little apartment tucked away out beyond the furthest edge of the Underground. He opened his door as far as the chain would allow, and looked out at me with flinty eyes. "Yes?"

"It's me," I said.

Cede didn't open the door.

He was a squat little man, in his seventies, with rubbery features, an elfin smile, and an accent that roamed the Highlands without settling. His hair had beat a retreat from his brow, and mustered reinforcements behind his ears.

I sighed. "Three of swords, Ace of wand, and the Hanged Man inverted."

Satisfied with the code, Cede stood up, beamed a radiant smile, and pulled open the door. "California! Why don't you come in for a cup of tea!"

"Thank you," I said, bracing myself for the fog of weed smoke and cat smell that saturated the flat.

Cede locked the door behind us, and hurried ahead, to put the kettle on. I lingered in the living room. There was a bong, coffee pot, and a dozen different books on the coffee table. A confusion of cats sprawled out over the sofa, half of them asleep, half of them looking stoned. There was an electric radiator in the fireplace, and the mantle was decorated by several decades of postcards and photographs.

Cede's obsession covered the walls. Most people had wallpaper, but Cede had newspaper clippings, magazine articles, and pages printed from the internet, tacked over every square inch, and connected by threads of red tape.

Cede collected impossible stories: The people who swore they saw Nelson Mandela's funeral years before he was released from prison, or that they saw films that don't exist. He collects stories of people who went to diners that weren't there the next day, or picked up hitch-hikers who vanished before they reached the next town. Where I saw tricks of the mind, the plastic nature of human memory, or people telling tall tales for attention, he saw evidence of other worlds, other histories, that bled into our own.

Cede didn't think Drift opened our minds to dreams. He thought it showed us something of the other worlds.

It was a harmless enough belief, and if one his discerning customers were expected to play along with. In his world he wasn't a dealer supplying a designer drug, he was a researcher, conducting a broad and deep survey of other worlds.

A few moments later he emerged with two mugs of tea, and scooted most the cats from the sofa.

"Now," he said, rummaging for his notebook, "what did you see?"

"Just Tanner," I said. "Working, as usual. He's looking...tired."

Cede nodded. "Did you hear the radio, see the news, anything that might be useful?"

"No," I said, regretfully. "It's a kitchen, they don't have that sort of thing."

Cede puffed out his cheeks. "I see."

"But," I said quietly, "I will probably pick up something on Friday."

"Oh?" He smiled. "Ah! Movie night!"

"They always gossip, and chat," I said. "And there might be a newspaper on the coffee table, or their laptop on..."

Cede nodded. "Good! Good!"

"If," I added meaningfully, "I can reach them."

Cede smiled. "I think that can be arranged. You always have such... interesting movies to talk about."

This was true. Apparently somewhere in the last eight years the Tanner of my dreams had run out of bad old movies to watch, and sometimes watched new ones. His Hollywood had weathered the sexual scandals of ours, and faced different ones of its own (which had Cede very excited, as he was trying to work out if the same things happened here, but had been covered up). As a result, his movies were... sometimes a little different, and sometimes a lot different to ours.

"He's still not dating," I said. "Not exactly. And... he does videos, on social stream. To advertise his restaurant. I haven't got to see them yet, but..."

Cede nodded. I don't think this was what he was interested in, but he was too polite to refuse any information.

I stopped talking. I had veered dangerously

close to Cede's way of thinking.

My grip clenched on my mug. My heart twisted.

Cede tapped his lips. "I don't suppose you can work out who won the cup final in his world?"

I nodded. Let's be honest, there wasn't much I wouldn't have agreed to.

"Usual price?" I asked, digging the cash from my pocket.

Twenty minutes later I was heading back to the city, aimless, adrift, and alone in the crowd, with nowhere to be and nothing to be doing.

My phone beeped. It was a number I didn't recognise. The Text however could only be read in a rolling Highland accent: *You are being followed. Bald man. Sunglasses.*

I stopped and looked around the crowded tube station. There were a sea of people, but none of them were bald, with sunglasses. Even so, my heart hammered in my chest.

"Dammit Cede!" I hissed, under my breath.

Maybe he did it deliberately. Maybe he let his paranoia infect others, to put them on edge, to want his product more.

Or maybe the kooky old geezer should not have been sampling his own wares.

It was Thursday, and the week was getting greyer.

Tanner's Empty Smile

I'd got pretty good at wearing the smile.

I wouldn't pretend I was any kind of celebrity, but sometimes I was, in small ways, recognised. Or, at the very least Fred was recognised, and I was the 'other one', from the videos. People don't care about me, as a chef, but when they meet the guy from the videos, they have certain expectations. When I was on screen, or being that guy, I had learned to wear a smile that was near enough genuine, that didn't look like I was a haunted ventriloquist dummy.

I might almost has passed for somebody you might want to talk to.

Almost.

I leant over the sink, staring into the mirror, trying to get the smile right.

There was a knock on the door. I knew it was Fred from the way she knocked.

"I'm okay," I said.

"It's just cooking, Tanner," Fred said. "Is anybody else in there?"

I looked at the stalls, they were empty. "Yeah, but… I'm okay."

She stepped into the toilet, and put a hand on my shoulder. "Tanner. We can do this. It's the same recipe, it's just cooking, we'll just be doing it in a studio. That's nothing."

"Except," I said, "it's a big deal."

"It's an audition and a screen test," Fred insisted. "It's not a big deal."

"You really want this job?" I asked. "To do our thing on TV?"

Fred took my hand in both of hers. "I do."

"Then," I said, quietly, "this is really, really, a big deal."

Fred put my hand to her cheek. "Are you okay?"

I nodded, and forced the smile on my lips.

Twenty minutes later we were in the studio, under the

glare of cameras, that were a lot bigger than the little ones we used for our videos were pointed at me on a simple kitchen set, white and brushed steel, arranged so there was a long worksurface on an elongated island, facing the cameras.

I tried not to think of the cameras being windows through which millions of people could watch us. It was just a test. We would cook a recipe, and be compared to who knows how many other potential presenters and then, the chances were, our tape would be discarded and forgotten.

The director told us to go, and the cameras rolled.

As soon as I started talking, and cooking something else took over. I didn't have to think. I just had to cook, and to perform, and both of those were a lot easier than real life. "Good morning, I'm Tanner."

"And I'm Fred," Fred said, with a smile. "And this is the perfect Sunday pudding. A fruit pie you can make with just a little effort, and perfect custard that will be silk smooth and full of flavour every single time." She turned from the camera and winked at me. "Or at least that's what he said, so if it goes wrong, blame him and open a tin."

It passed in a blur. Fred showed the cameras her brilliant quick-blitz pastry that could be made in a few moments with a good food processor. When she left it to rest I stepped around her, describing the easiest way to peel, skin, and slice the fruits, adding them to the filling.

"The sugar is a little sweetness kick," I said, staring into the camera, "but we don't need much because the fruits are all going to supplying the sweetness. The flour is just enough to coat them, and thicken the juices into a nice fruity gravy, like a jam."

Fred laughed. "Are you sure? I remember when you said that about those apples my wife grew."

I tossed an apple over my shoulder, and she caught it, taking a bite.

"Oh, bloody Hell!" She said, approvingly. "Right. They only need how to see to chop one of each of the fruit. Repeat, repeat, repeat, until all the fruit, is in the bowl…" She winked at the camera, and rolled out the pastry. "Some simple tips for not making a mess of this. Lots of flour, on the board and on the rolling pin, and now look at this…"

I only interrupted to 'borrow' some flour to coat the fruit. By the time my filling was assembled the pie dish had been lined, the pastry rolled out, and the lattice top was ready to go on. I filled the pie, Fred put the top on, and put it in the oven.

Fred pointed a wooden spoon at me. "Custard. Does anybody still make custard? You can get some pretty good stuff from the supermarket these days."

"Better than mine?" I asked.

Fred wobbled her hand in a so-so kind of gesture, and gave me a teasing smile.

"You can't claim the overload if it's in a carton," I warned her. "Nobody leaves any spare."

"Oh, go on then!" Fred laughed. "How many eggs?"

She tossed them from one end of the set to the other. I caught them, cracked them, and separated the yolks all one handed. The last two she threw in quick succession son I had to catch them one in each hand.

"You do know," I warned her, "what I would tell you if I found you larking like that in my kitchen at work?"

"Yes," Fred answered. "I also know this isn't your kitchen, it's my set, so can you guess what I'm about to tell you?"

I turned my back on her carry on with my work. "The viewers at home will have to tune in for the post-watershed edition to find out."

Fred sidled up to me, and watched over my shoulder. "I'm sorry, is this distracting?"

Despite Fred's games, I managed to keep smiling, keep talking, and to show the cameras how to make a rich, velvet soft custard, without it looking too much sweat and bother to put people off. I decanted it into a jug, and let Fred eat the excess from the pan.

"My sister," I said, once she had a mouthful, "is supposed to casually enquire if this is the same crème Anglaise I would make for filling sweet pastries and tarts.

Yes. If you let it set, and eat it cold it sets thick enough to slice, and won't ooze away."

"Can't talk," Fred said. "So good!"

The cameras cut, and we were allowed off the set. I marched outside, and took some fresh air. My stomach knotted, and bile filled the back of my throat. I swallowed it back before I could throw up, and loosened my tunic.

It was one of the producers who found me.

"You'll get used to this," she said, passing me a bottle of water. "Are you okay?"

"Oh, don't worry, if this hasn't ruined our chance, I can promise you I will never be like this in front of a camera."

"Don't worry, we are going to look at the tapes, have a discussion, I think your names are going to come up, and either way, we will let you know."

It looked like Fred was told the same thing. When I found in the studio offices, she was bouncing around like somebody had put twenty pence in her. She was clinging to the arm of Li, her wife, with a big grin and bright eyes.

Li smiled at me, cupped my chin. "You were brilliant. Almost as brilliant as my little star."

Li was short, slight, and of a nimble build, with almond skin and chocolate hair. She had a delicate, elfin beauty, and looked like she could be swept away by a good sneeze, but Fred was always her little something. Her little beauty, her little star, or angel. I loved it, not least because of the way it made Fred's cheeks blossom.

We made it back to the coast just in time for the evening's work.

The past hit me as I was chopping vegetables. I don't know what stirred the unwanted memories, maybe the sound, or some smell, or something in the rhythm of the knife. Maybe it was nothing at all.

Dad was always too close to my memories.

I could remember Mum, or Callie, if I tried, if I closed my eyes, and drew them out, picturing their image, holding the feel of their embrace, in my mind, the little details would all follow. With Dad it was different.

With Dad I could smell his sweat, and feel the callouses on the fingers closing around my throat, if I wanted it or not. I felt the pop of my ribs as he broke them, and the taste of the rug as he stamped on me.

It was never a single moment that would bubble up. It would be a tangled skein of barbed thoughts and fractured history.

I remembered the moment I knew he was going to hit me for the first time. I was twelve. He didn't think I was boyish enough. I didn't like football, I didn't chase girls, or at least not the way he expected, and he thought cooking wasn't something a boy should like. It was close to Christmas and he had been to his office party, got a little drunk, and talked himself into confronting me about it.

He caught me alone in my bedroom. "You know Tanner, if you carry on like that, people are going to think you are gay."

I sat on my bed, and gave him a blank look. It didn't seem much of a deal what people assumed about me. My failure to launch into a vigorous defence condemned me in his eyes. Too late, I told him I wasn't. It didn't matter. I could see his expression set to disgust. It didn't matter what I said.

He was going to beat the gay out of me.

For a while I was too afraid to tell anybody what was going on. Dad would make jokes about how useless I was at sport, or boxing, throwing "playful" punches at me just often enough that people would laugh off any bruises they saw. He was a funny sort, he just didn't know his own strength.

I don't know if anybody bought the act, or if they just thought silence was becoming, when it came to wondering how he treated his own kids.

I wasn't going to tell. I couldn't.

All the time he was hitting me, he wasn't thinking about Fred. He was noticing who she took second glances at. Who she longed for.

Then one Christmas (it was always worst around then), he punched me to floor, and just kept stamping down, until my ribs broke, and I passed out. I could have died then, but that didn't make what followed, Dad going to trial, custody agreements being replaced by restraining orders, Dad's sentencing in prison, any easier. There was guilt. Guilt because I had hidden it from Mum for so long, guilt because after everything Dad still noticed Fred's crushes. Guilt, because, despite everything else, he was my Dad, and it seemed my fault he was in prison.

My head filled with insults, all the things he had screamed and roared and spat at me, as he kicked me, or throttled me, and all the things he had grumbled at me when he knew he didn't have to say a word.

I stopped.

The knife slipped from my hands. I stepped away from the board, and grabbed my head. I gasped for breath, and held back the tears. Anger and hatred burned in my heart. It boiled in my heart, and knotted my lungs. My fingers curled to fists, and dug into my palms, until my knuckles bleached. I drowned in a maelstrom of white noise memories.

"You in there, Chef?" Squeak asked, snapping his fingers.

I hit reality with a bump. "What?"

Squeak stared at me. "Movie night. What are we watching?"

"Ana's choice," I said, behind a hollow smile, pretending all was well.

Two of Li's sisters, Ana and Rose, worked front of house, as a hostess and at the bar, respectively. They were both great, and they both threw themselves whole heartedly into starting the weekend right after an always busy Friday shift.

"Am I making burgers or dogs?" He asked.

I shook my head. "I'll cook. Chilli and Chips."

Squeak bustled on his way.

I fixed the mask of normality in place, and started chopping.

Squeak doubled back. "Are we going to need some bubbly?"

I shrugged. "I have no idea how long producers take to choose presenters."

Squeak shrugged. "Hey… it can't hurt right?"

"Are you paying for it?" I asked.

"Beer it is!" Squeak decided with gusto.

*

Friday passed in a blur of work. The day's special was a slow cooked, smoky chili, on rice, or on a burger, and before we cleared down and scrubbed the kitchen, I made sure we had considerable mountain of thrice cooked chips being kept warm. With the kitchen clean, the doors locked, the lights dimmed, and as much prep as possible done ahead of time to make Saturday that little bit easier, the whole staff sat in the booths around the edge of the restaurant, along with some of their friends, armed with cold drinks, and piles of chili on chips, to giggle and natter along as I set a film playing.

Ana, the youngest of the Blossom sisters, had chosen a cartoon to watch. An adventure yarn with knights, princesses, and a comedy goat. The goat didn't speak but Ana, Li, and Rose were all determined to fill in it's dialogue, in gruff cod-Yorkshire accents.

I lingered serving the food until everybody was settled, then found myself a quiet booth to myself.

I couldn't get into the film, so I checked my dating apps. I had a whole slew of thank you, but no thank you messages. I swiped past countless faces, looking at them, but not seeing anybody.

A cold breeze brushed against me from nowhere. It carried a sweet, floral, slightly spiced bouquet of perfume, like a rose garden after the rain. Callie's perfume.

My entire body tensed, my cheeks burned red, goosepimples covered my skin. My heart stuck in my throat and refused to beat.

A soft breath brushed against my neck.

My heart shattered.

I ran from the restaurant, carried by panic and tears, to the seafront.

CALLIE'S GHOST

Friday I spent looking around the exhibition I had fund-raised for. I didn't throw my weight around, or call ahead. I queued for tickets like anybody else and saw it the right way. It was kind of my undercover mission, checking that the promises that were easy to keep in private showings with ample warning, were kept day to day.

I almost got away with it too, but one of the managers recognised me before I could reach the gift shop. We went and had a chat by my favourite mummies, and he made the mistake of telling me about the book he was writing.

Kid-friendly versions of some of my favourite myths and legends, illustrated with photographic dioramas made with little wargame figures. I managed to convince him to give me a look, in exchange for an evening meal somewhere impressive.

One of Adam's Personal Assistants was quick to find a table that certainly impressed me.

Dinner was nice, and the company was fine. Once I put twenty pence in the guy he wouldn't stop talking about history, then his writing, then the photographs for the book (which were absolutely beautiful), then more about the little model soldiers than I ever wanted to know. I wasn't going to stop him talking about them. It was nice to see somebody get on that roll you can only hit when there's genuine passion for a project.

He wanted to talk more over coffee, but it was Friday night, and I had somewhere else to be. I got him to wait with me for my car, then promised I would check back in on his project when I had time.

I got back to the apartment in ample time, and

freed myself from my bra, for the blessed relief of a comfy tee and pyjama shorts. I freed my hair from the pins and clips that bound it, poured a wine, dimmed the lights, and sprawled out over the sofa, decanting one of the crystals from my pill bottle.

It melted on my tongue, slowly easing me down into hazy warmth and mellow relaxation. I closed my eyes, and let myself sink down into the Dream.

Tanner was about ready for movie night, scrubbing the counters with his steam gun, his brow set, and his lips pursed. I put a hand on his shoulder. His muscles were like steel rope under his cold, plastic skin. Even the steam was ice cold and full of shivers, at least to me.

"Hey," I whispered, "what's wrong?"

One of the pretty young women from his staff, with dusky skin and brown hair, lurked in the corner of the kitchen. She was dressed in her uniform of black shirt, and charcoal trousers lurked in the doorway. "I'm not trying to be rude," she said, "but if you and Fred are both going to be away more…"

Tanner looked at her. "Rose, our chances of being picked up for the show are pretty slim."

"Yeah, but… If you were, maybe I could help with managing the restaurant?" She asked, nervously. "I mean, if you, or Fred could show me how to help out…"

Tanner's expression softened the way it did when he was turning thoughts around to look at them from all angles. "That would be a brilliant idea. I should talk to Fred about it, but…"

"I asked Fred," the woman, Rose, said with a smile as cute as a button. "She said you handled promotions or firings."

Tanner sighed. "Okay. I'll see what I can do."

Rose lit up bright, and skipped off out of the kitchen.

Tanner leant on the counter. His smile faltered,

and faded.

"Hey!" I said, stroking his arm. "You might be on TV? Why are you on TV? What's going on?" I grinned, and stepped close. "Hey…" I spotted the food awaiting movie night. "That smells so good!"

Of course, he didn't hear me. He took a bowl of chili out into he restaurant floor, and started ladling it over chunky fries, garnished with salsa, cheese, and sour cream. He took the last bowl for himself. Squeak set a projector running, and a cartoon I did not recognise shimmied to life on the screen, I joined Tanner in his quiet little booth.

I snuggled as best I could against his arm. "Okay, if this is a dream, I do not want to know what dark corner of my subconscious this film comes from."

Tanner picked at his food, and flicked through a dating app. I rested my head on his shoulder, as he flicked past a few profiles, without really looking at them.

"Hang on," I said, squeezing at his arm. "She's cute."

He kept on flicking past.

"Are you even trying?" I asked, with a chuckle. "How about this one, she's a little older than you might… nope. Nope? Really?"

I let out a long sigh.

Tanner froze and tensed. His expression went pale.

"Tanner?" I asked.

He looked around, his eyes… distant and haunted. He stared right at me, or through me. I waved a hand by his eyes, but he didn't react.

"Have you seen a ghost?" I stroked his neck. "Me?"

The muscles were taut, and his pulse was pounding under his frost cold skin.

Tanner lunged past me in a flailing mess of gangly limbs, as he ran for the door, and vanished into the *street. I bolted after him, running as hard as the Dream would let me, as he flew from the high street, across the main road, over the seawall and down onto the pebble beaches. Fred was quicker, breezing past me to catch her brother in a hug.*

"Tanner!" She said, softly. "What the actual?"

I lingered as close as I dared to their embrace. "Was it me? Did he sense me?"

"I can't go back," Tanner said, gasping for breath, panic making him pale and quivering. "She was there."

"Who?" Fred asked slowly.

Tanner swallowed. "California."

"You saw California?" Fred asked, carefully.

"No. I... felt her. Her perfume was there, and she breathed on my neck, like she used to when we were... for the little while we were..." He rubbed his head. "It was her."

"It was me!" I laughed. "I did this!"

Fred nodded. "You have no idea how many times

I could have sworn Mum was right over my shoulder, about to touch my hair like she used to."

"This wasn't like that," He muttered. "This was more like…" He reached up and brushed something under his hair. A scar. "More like that night."

Fred put his head to her shoulder and clung to him. "Okay. Okay. So… maybe its something. It's probably nothing, but we can get a doctor to check it's not… something."

"It was her," Tanner insisted. "Again."

"Again?" I spluttered over the word. "Again?"

"I did see her that night," Tanner insisted. "Just before… it happened. I saw her, floating, drowning, and… and after…"

"You saw me?" I patted his shoulder. "I saw you! The night I almost… Oh… shit! I saw you, and you saw me?"

"Okay." Fred smiled. "I believe you. I believe… that night she wanted to say goodbye, and tonight

maybe she wanted you to know she was okay. Right?"

"Or," Tanner muttered, "she blames me."

"Blames you?" Fred asked.

"Why would I blame him?" I squawked. "What the Hell Tanner?"

"Well, when we were fighting, she said… all the same stuff Dad used to say. What if…" Tanner sagged in her arms, like gravity had been turned up a few notches. "What if it's true? If I'd been less spineless, and pathetic, and… actually showed a backbone for a moment? Just a moment? If…it'd actually been a fight. I mean…"

"Oh." Fred sighed. "You think history would have changed if she went to Venice believing you were even more of an arsehole?" Her expression turned fierce. "Look at me! You… you are nothing like Dad. Nothing. You will never, ever, give that human skid mark the satisfaction of believing he had any kind of a point."

Tears rolled down my cheeks. "Tanner, I was

always getting on the train. I thought you believed any

of what I said, it could only make it harder."

Fred held him as he cried.

"You idiot!" I groaned, softly. "I love you."

He didn't hear that.

I let myself surface from the dream, and lay on

the sofa, crying for a long time.

Callie Haunted

Cede watched me from under his living blanket of cats, stroking one of his tortoise shell tabbies behind the ears. "The film sounds interesting, of course…"

"Not the film," I said. "Tanner."

"Your… ex?" He asked.

"He felt me." I held up a finger. "That isn't how the Dream is meant to work."

"Ah," Cede raised an eyebrow. "But you don't think it is real, do you? Why couldn't you dream that he felt your touch?"

"Then, why now?" I sipped my tea. "Why not… when I first started Drifting?"

"Perhaps you think about him differently now," Cede said. "Eight years is a long time, and I do not think that for the first five years, until you came to me, you thought of him at all."

"I did," I admitted, although I knew I hadn't, enough.

I was in a bad place, and it was too painful. I told myself I was so in love with Adam I was doing the noble thing, the good thing, by letting go of my ex, of his memory, and not... turning my back on friends.

"We always want what can never, or should never, be ours," Cede mused.

"And assuming," I said, quietly, "that your theories are right, and..." I trailed off a moment. Did I want to voice this idea? Did I want to torture myself with it? "If there really is a world out there where somebody did the decent thing, and let me swap my life for his, then how can I have...how can he..."

Cede grinned. "Do you know what the most exciting words a scientist can say are?"

I shrugged. "Why yes I do have handcuffs and a feather duster?"

"No." He mimed with his hands. "I. Don't. Know."

"You have no idea?" I asked. "At all?"

"I am," Cede said brightly, "thoroughly excited."

I sipped my tea again. "Can I dream things I don't know?"

Cede frowned at me. "Like, what?"

"Tanner never spoke about his father." I chose my words carefully. "I knew his mother was dead, and I assumed she had been a single parent, but… after the dream, I couldn't sleep. I couldn't do anything. So… I spent what was left of the night looking stuff up online, and… Tanner's dad was in prison for nearly a decade, for beating Tanner, my Tanner, my best friend, so bad that he broke Tanner's ribs." She stopped. "He thought one of his kids was gay. Hopefully he had no idea how wrong he was."

"Was?" Cede asked.

My throat was suddenly dry. "He's gone. A few years after Tanner passed, he overdosed in a hovel, and wasn't found for a few days. It seemed pretty deliberate."

"And in their world?" Cede asked.

I paused. "They talk like he's still around. He made another choice."

Cede nodded. "Maybe you read about the father, somewhere. You overheard something you forgot about, or wasn't aware of. Maybe part of you wasn't as good at letting go as you wanted to believe."

"Or?" I asked.

"Or you saw something in the dream you can't know," Cede said, "because it wasn't just a dream."

That thought scared me. I longed for it to be

true, but it scared me.

"Okay," I said, quietly, afraid of disturbing a notion as fine as spider silk, "if I was seeing his world, if he's real... how can he feel me? I thought we could only observe, not interfere."

"That is," Cede agreed, "the usual nature of our dreams." He tapped his lips. "But... there are those who have experienced the other timelines naturally, who have slipped between worlds, in small ways, or for little moments... Perhaps you are open to such influences, or perhaps he is... sensitive to your presence?"

"Could he hear me?" I asked.

Cede looked at me. "He isn't your friend. His life has run a different course."

"He lost his Callie," I said, gently, "like I lost my Tanner. He... deserves to know she didn't blame him."

"Maybe she did," Cede said.

"And?" I stared at him. "If I can offer him peace, he deserves it."

"It won't change what happened to your Tanner," Cede said, warningly.

I flinched under his flinty gaze. "I hardly think that excuses me from showing this other man kindness."

"No!" Cede's eyes brightened. "No. I don't suppose it would."

"So..." My heart stuttered. "Can I tell him?"

Cede shook his head. "I'm sorry."

*

I rode the tube in a sullen, grey, mood, my heart aching. I checked my phone a dozen times, but there was no word from Adam. As my train slid into the station, I hopped off, and made my way through the crowd.

Somebody followed me.

I got a glimpse, just a vague glimpse of a bald

man, in a long coat and sunglasses. I glanced back, and he ducked down a side passage.

I ran home as fast as I could.

*

Adam was there when I got home, sitting in the lounge, his head in his hands. He looked up at me, his brow furrowed, his expression deathly. "I couldn't reach you."

I looked at the two other men in our apartment. Security guys in black polo shirts and khaki trousers. Both had tattoos on their wrists. Private Security. Adam had used them before.

I sat beside him, and squeezed him in a hug. "I thought you were in Texas."

"I was," he whispered. "Then I discovered somebody had hacked the Smart Hub, and made it listen into us." He tapped his watch, and played a file on the smart speakers dotted about the apartment. "Listen."

It was my own voice that spoke. "Tanner, I was always getting on the train. I thought you believed any of what I said, it could only make it harder. You idiot! I love you."

"Somebody heard that?" I asked. "Adam, there was somebody following me. A bald man. Glasses. I only caught a glimpse."

"Okay." Adam said. His voice strained. "I couldn't reach you."

I smiled. "I was seeing a friend."

"A dealer?" He waved the security guys away. "I mean, obviously you have been Drifting. Was it a dealer?"

I nodded. "Adam. It's not illegal."

"No." He stroked my cheek. "That doesn't mean it hasn't become a problem."

"It's not..." I looked at him. "It's not what you think."

His eyes filled with worries. "You Drift to see

Tanner."

I nodded. "But not like… You don't have to be jealous."

"Jealous?" Adam shook his head. "No. You have a way to see a world that still has him in it. To tell him stuff you never got to say. I can see the appeal." He swallowed. "You haven't told him about… stuff I said…"

He trailed off. I knew the conversation he meant. Back when the accident had put him in a dark place, and he was too macho to admit how bad he needed help, he had staggered into our little French cottage and screamed at me about how 'that fucking English turd' was going to steal me away, and Adam couldn't compete with a dead man. Apparently, the last thing Tanner did 'before he had the good grace to headbutt a speeding car' was play a move that Adam wished beyond wish, that he could have thought of first. What better way,

Adam demanded to know, to prove you were the man I should be with, than to have the chivalry and humility to step aside graciously, and actually offer to help the other guy win. What could be more worthy?

He had kept talking until he was hoarse with tears, before he shut up long enough for me to tell him I loved him.

Back in the here and now, I put a finger on his lips. "No. If I did, he wouldn't hear me."

"But..." Adam looked at me. "You were talking to him."

I nodded. "I talk for me. It... helps."

"Are you sure?" Adam spoke softly. "I can see the appeal. Trust me, if I could see one of my uncles again, I would, but how much are you doing this? How often?"

"Mostly for movie nights," I whispered.

"Oh." He drew a breath. "I think maybe we

need to get you some help. This… isn't healthy."

"I know," I whispered. "I just need a little longer. I just need…"

"Yeah." He stroked my hair. "I know what that is like. A few more hits, to get you through the next few days, or weeks, or past the next milestone? And then the next. And then a few more? Drink did that to me, and you helped me clear my head. I need to do the same to you." He hugged me close. "My demons tore us apart too often. I'm not letting either of us get hurt again."

"You don't understand…"

"Callie," he said firmly. "Somebody hacked us, and you said he followed you. I need to do this to keep you safe. Please."

My heart sank. "Just a little more. Please. I am so close…"

"Close?" Adam asked.

"I…" My throat filled with cinders and smoke.

"I can save him this time."

Adam stared into my eyes, his soul wounded to the core. "I'm so sorry Callie, but the sooner you see that you can't, the better. There isn't a This Time. There's a dream. Just a dream." He stroked his cheek. "It's okay. We are going to make this work. I promise."

I shook my head. "You want me to lose him again?"

Adam flinched from the words. "It isn't like that. He isn't real Callie. He's nothing but wishful thinking and a legally dubious high."

"He's real to me," I whispered.

Adam stood, and walked over to the kitchen. "Perhaps he was."

"Was?" I asked.

Adam didn't answer. He tapped the screen of his watch, and frowned. "I have a message here I have to handle. We can talk about this later."

From his tone of voice, I knew his mind was made up.

Tanner Lost

Weeks later, Li came with me to a supplier I knew in London for some ingredients. We drove up in my van, and parked in a back street of Whitechapel. Ravi was my wholesaler of choice for spices. Nobody imported chili peppers that tasted like his, or paprika that had been smoked the way his uncle made it. We loading up on some nice big bags, when my phone rang.

"Hey," Fred said, almost laughing. "We got it."

"Got what?" I asked.

"Got what?" She squawked. "The show! They want us for the pilot!"

"Yes!" Li punched the air. "Tell her we are booking a venue up here. I know a place."

"A venue for what?" I asked, cautiously.

"Party," Li said. "Right?"

"Right!" Fred agreed. "Brilliant! Yes! A party!"

I paid Ravi and sighed. "Want to come to a party Rav?"

The merchant grinned. "I would!"

Li and I drove out to a large industrial looking building by the Thames, a good way from the centre of the City.

"This," I said, "does not look like a venue."

"It's more impressive on the inside," she promised. "Wait here. I need to go speak to the management."

With that, Li hopped out the car and ran to one of the houses. The front door was opened by a short older man, with hair thinning on top, but heavy behind his ears. He greeted her in a familiar manner, and they ducked inside.

I listened to the radio, and checked my dating app, without joy.

Something caught my eye. A car pulled away without anybody getting in it. I glanced at it, out of idle curiosity. The drab silver car slowed as it passed my van.

My father stared out at me, over his sunglasses.

He had shaved his head, and lost weight, but it was him. He smiled, but there was no joy or warmth to his smile.

In the blink of an eye, he was accelerating away, far faster than the speed limit, and squealing around the corner.

I sat rigid, unmoving, for several long minutes, until Li came bouncing from the house, and hopped in the van. The glow of her smile cooled.

Li stared at me. "Are you okay?"

I shook my head.

*

Fred kept telling me that seeing Dad, if I had seen him, was probably just a coincidence. She smiled brightly, and told me not to worry about it, but she still had new security lights fitted around the restaurant and her bungalow. She still insisted on giving me a lift home every night rather than letting me walk.

The morning she picked me up for our first recording, she still had that worried little twitch to her smile that she had worn as a kid.

"It's because of the show," Fred told me, firmly. "I've been getting enough venom from weirdos on the internet, as it is. I'd rather be ready for the trolls that national television is going to dredge up, okay?"

I rubbed the back of my neck. "Have you been on my dating profile?"

"Your password was too easy to guess," she said, in a Big Sister kind of way. "You need to look at that."

"Did you add 'As Seen On TV' to my profile?"

Fred grinned. In the backseat Li was laughing into her hands.

I cleared my throat. "You… didn't look at any of my messages, right?"

"No!" They said, together.

"Although…" Li leant forwards, tucking her head over the shoulder of my chair. "I have a few friends coming to the party tonight, that you might want to meet."

"Oh. Right…" I smiled. "Would they want to meet me?"

Li shot Fred a mischievous look. "Maybe we should let them try the food first."

"Definitely!" Fred agreed. "Let the food do the talking…" She chewed her lip. "Do we have time to take a look at the venue first?"

Li nodded. "Yes!"

"Not really…" I moaned.

"Outvoted!" The girls declared together.

I sank into my seat.

*

The venue was an old electrical substation that had been adopted as a performing arts space. The walls were a distinctive yellow brick, the floor was dyed and polished concrete, as slick as an ice rink. Overhead a forest of chains and cables hung from the arched ceiling, holding lightbulbs of every shape and size, from tiny fairy lights, to huge industrial bulbs. The overall impression was of a golden glow, rather than a dazzling glare. There was a stage at one end, and a bar at the other. The furniture and décor was a patchwork of wood, salvaged and reclaimed, some from an old pub, some from factories and churches. The booths and tables were all made from old doors.

Li walked across the dancefloor, her arms held out. "They say you can set up your kitchen over there, and the DJ will be over there, and…"

"It's perfect," Fred promised. "Isn't it perfect?"

"Is…" I swallowed. "Is this what you want? A big party? Here?"

Fred nodded. "It is."

"Then, it is perfect," I promised. "Did anybody give Squeak the postcode? I mean, if he doesn't bring the van…"

Fred put her hands on my cheeks. "It's going to be fine. Everything is sorted."

I nodded. "Okay. Sorry. Nerves."

Li glanced at me. She had a thoughtful look in her eye.

"Sorry," I mumbled again.

Fred kissed my forehead. "Can we go and be famous now?"

*

I stood on the set, my heart racing, my throat dry,

suddenly unsure if I even knew how to cook, or talk, let alone how to do both. Fear bubbled through my nerves, and stamped on my bladder. I drew a breath.

"Okay," the director said, "adjust those lights…better… and we will go in three two one…"

In an instant the performer part of my mind took control, and I was smiling at the camera with an easy confidence I didn't feel.

"Good morning!" I said, happily. "I'm Tanner."

"And I'm Fred!" Fred beamed at the camera. "This is going to be the perfect meat ball sub. I fell in love with these, when I visited New York on my gap year. Mum and Tanner came to visit me for a couple of weeks, and I made them travel halfway across the city with me, in search of this one food truck, that did a great sandwich. It was a bit of a pricy habit, so out of necessity I learned to make a pretty good meatball, and a really good sauce, for a really low price. They work great with a handful of pasta, but we are going to show you a few little tricks to make a divinely decadent treat, best served with a side of fries, and lots of napkins."

I kicked things off by getting the rich tomato sauce going, with fried onions and garlic, cheap tinned tomatoes, and some basic ingredients. I got it bubbling away on the stove. Fred took the baton and did the heart of the recipe, the meat balls. A little chopping, a little blending, and a little work, and the meatballs were roasting in the oven.

I blended down the sauce, and showed off a few of the tricks diners used to make even the cheapest rolls taste amazing, by cramming in as many calories as possible, smothering everything in butter, cheese, or both, and frying it all, every step of the way.

We gave quantities per person, and cooked in bulk, enough to ensure the final shot would be of the production crew all getting to try some of the sandwich.

We did a few more takes, and some detail shots on the method, close ups on the knife, or the mix. Then we reset the stage and did a segment showing off a quick and easy way of making pasta, that we served in a light, zesty, vegetable sauce. I made it vegan with some courgette spaghetti.

Sometimes when I remember it, it felt like a few moments. Sometimes it felt like it took an eternity.

*

We celebrated that night with the party.

I took care of the food. Squeak could have gone to hang out at the bar, but he insisted on staying for a while. It soon became clear when I saw the way he smiling at some of the guests, and making a point of telling them about the food, or at least in the suave little smile he had when they glanced back for a second look.

Most the guests were friends of Fred and Li's, or friends of friends. It was hard to keep track. There were a few people I knew, and a lot I didn't, but Fred seemed to know everybody. She shook every hand, had a little smile, and managed to get a laugh from everyone.

Ana and Rose hung at a booth, but would stop by to keep us plied with beer.

The music was loud, but not too loud to hear. The

crowd was louder.

I sipped beer from a bottle, and choked on small talk.

After a while, once everybody had burgers, or vegan-dogs, or a couple of both, the cheer and ambience in the venue seemed to give it a soft and fuzzy atmosphere. The lights blurred into a rainbow of colours, and gravity loosened its grip on me.

I stared at the embers of the wood burning in the grill, hypnotised by the way their light seemed to flutter like butterflies.

Li shook my shoulder. "Tanner. Are you okay?"

I smiled at her. "I honestly don't know. Is it kind of… swirly in here?"

"Oh no." She stared into my eyes. "Tanner look at me a moment mate. "She took my beer and sniffed the bottle. "Have you been… experimenting?"

"It's okay." Squeak eased her away from me. "It's nothing illegal. Just Drift. It won't get him too high, or get him in trouble. It just… loosens you up for the weekend.

Unwinds the stress.”

“And how,” Fred demanded, appearing from nowhere, “do you know that? Did you spike his drink?”

“No!” Squeak pointed at himself. “I spiked my own drink, then gave him the wrong one!”

Li smiled. “He’ll be fine. I’ll take him to a booth, and sit with him. He can drink water.”

I nodded. “Good idea.” The world wobbled the wrong way. I stopped shaking my head. “Sorry.”

“It’s okay,” Li assured me.

We walked around the edge of the dancefloor. A guy in a dinner jacket, one that was dark red silk, rather than black, stepped in my way.

“Sorry,” I said, too late.

He smashed into me, ice cold, and hard as granite, barging me into the dancers as though he hadn’t even seen me. Li caught me before I could fall, her arms on my sides.

“Thank you,” I muttered.

Li nodded, her grip relaxing, as she stepped closer,

guiding me into a gentle sway to match the music.

"I don't dance," I warned her.

"I can see that," she agreed. "You don't mind?"

The world still felt too light, but it was warm and safe, more so in her arms, afloat on a river of music.

"No. I don't mind."

"Good." She put her cheek to mine. "I have a wife, and I have sisters, but a big brother is still a novelty to me. I like it. I should make use of it more often."

We danced until one song faded into another. She dragged me off the dancefloor.

A woman, shorter than me, plumper, and a few years younger suddenly blocked my way. I skidded aside to avoid her.

"Sorry!" I said, holding up my hands. "Entirely my..." My words trailed off.

The woman looked up at me, her eyes widening, and her lips parting, in confusion.

She was a decade older, and was dressed in

an extravagant ball gown, her hair was more restrained from the wild curls, and her features had refined a little with age, but…

But… that was impossible.

"I'm sorry," I whispered.

"Me too," Callie agreed, dazed. She grabbed me in a hug. "Hi."

I wanted to say 'hi' too, but I was too busy holding her close, crying into her shoulder.

I kissed her forehead, and in the blink of an eye, **she vanished, dissolving into nothingness. I pitched over, hugging empty air, and slammed face first into the floor.**

It wasn't concrete, it was stained glass. Above me, instead of the forest of lightbulbs were flashing rainbow squares of light, and around me, instead of a swarm of friends-of-friends were walls of stained glass waterfalls, and elegant men and women, in formal suits and ball gowns, dancing to some

seriously retro music.

Callie Betwixt

Another weekend, and another fund raiser.

This one was worse though: Adam had volunteered us both to help out. He didn't say so, but it felt pretty obvious he wanted to be busy, thinking about something other than finding time to drift.

I was happy to be back in my real life, but… the more I tried not to think about the Dream, the more I found myself wondering if Tanner was working through his deals, or on television, or…

"I said," Adam repeated, "what do you think?"

The building was completely different on the inside. On the outside the former electrical substation had been a cathedral of aged yellow bricks, and rusty industrial chic. On the inside it was entirely clad in stained glass. The floor, ceiling and walls were covered in colourful patterns of blues and greens, lit from behind to give the impression of moving water, cascading waterfalls and a rippling pool. The bar, tables, and booths were all frosted glass painted with changing lights.

Our bodyguards lurked near the doorways.

I stood, mesmerised. "It's beautiful."

"The band," Adam said, "will be over there, the display about the Project and its works along that wall, and everybody can dance the night away. The Project gets to spread word, and draw in donations, and the club gets a lot of good publicity, looking... You called it beautiful, right?"

I nodded. "Is it ours?"

"It belongs to a company, that is ours," Adam said. He hugged me. "Do you think you can make this work?"

"Sure." I looked around. "I just need a bar, catering, a band, and... a display about the Project.

Great."

He kissed my cheek. "I know you've got this."

"Want to go to the museum later?" I asked. "To… pretend to be interested when I tell you all about the Book of the Dead?"

He winced. "I would, but if you have this in hand…"

"You have a thing?" I asked.

He nodded. "I have a thing."

*

A few days later, I was shopping for my ball gown. I had a place I liked to go, near Carnaby Street. Ross, my polo-shirted bodyguard stood in the corner of the shop, trying not to look bored as I talked for ages with Melissa, over two cups of tea, and some finger cakes.

"I know it's a rushed job," I said.

"No…" Melissa smiled. "It's a challenge, but I will make it work. You, my dear, will be divine."

I shook her hand, and smiled at Ross. "Hey, how about lunch? My treat for putting up with this."

"It's my job, ma'am," he reminded me.

"I know!" I leant closer. "But I know an Italian place, and if you have to watch over me, you might as well try the food. You will love it."

He smiled. "As long as its in the line of duty."

We went a few streets to the place I knew, and we had a lunch as amazing as promised. Ross didn't talk much. I don't know if he liked to keep a professional difference, or just didn't get on with me, but he never talked much.

Maybe he was just the strong silent type.

"I…" I cleared my throat. "I have to go and… powder my nose."

Ross nodded.

I stepped away from the table and into the powder room. It was empty and I had my choice of stalls. I picked the corner and closed the door. It was slammed back open, before I had a chance to lock it. The bald man with the sunglasses loomed into the cubicle. His hand shot out and covered my mouth.

"No!" He shushed me. "No. Don't scream. I… I'm not here to hurt you. I am here to give you what you want."

I shoved him back, away from me. He bounced off the sink, with a yelp of pain.

"Ross!" I screamed, running for the door. "Ross!"

"No!" The bald man tackled me, and we crashed to the tiled floor. He pinned me down, his arm across my throat. "You want to see my son. I will let you see him. All you have to do is promise to make him fall for you again, so I can ruin his life."

"What?" I gasped.

He pushed down on my throat.

My heart lurched through the gears, and my breath burned in my throat. Nightmare memories of deep Venice waters swallowed me, as I fought for breath.

The bald man flicked a syringe from his pocket. "This will not hurt."

The bathroom door burst open, and Ross barged in. He grabbed the bald man and hurled him away from me. The bald man crashed into the cubicle and slammed the door.

Ross kicked the door open, ripping latch from the wood in a shower of splinters.

The cubicle was empty.

"What," Ross demanded, "the actual?"

I gagged for breath.

*

That night, after the hours of speaking to the Police, of giving statements, of having doctors inspect the bump on the back of the head, and checking me over, I did not sleep. Adam lay beside me, stroking my hair.

"It can't have been Tanner's father," Adam said. "He's…"

"Dead?" I asked.

"You hit your head pretty bad," Adam reminded me.

"He vanished in a toilet cubicle," I said, quietly.

"So…" Adam frowned. "He was a ghost?"

I didn't answer.

"Have you been using?" Adam asked.

"I promised not to," I said, bluntly. "For you."

Adam squeezed me. "You know I have to ask."

I looked up at him. "Do you believe me?"

"I believe that you believe?" He offered.

"Do you?" I asked, watching his eyes.

His eyes flicked to one side, just like they always used to, when we were little more than kids, on-again and off-again, and he was going to tell me he hadn't made a pass at another woman.

"You don't," I whispered. "You think I'm lying?"

"No." He stared into my eyes. "I think you are trying very hard to believe it, because you need to, but I think you know this is the Drift talking."

"And was Ross drifting too?" I demanded.

He sighed, conceding that point.

"I'll sleep on the sofa," I said, rolling out of bed.

"But…"

I took my hoodie, and a pillow, and stomped out to the living room.

*

Tensions eased after a few days, as my fear dissipated, and Adam made a point of putting his arms around me more often.

As we drove to the charity gala he sidled up to

me in the back of the car.

"You don't have to do this," he whispered.

"I know." I gave him a smile. "Weird as it feels, if I don't it would be like… that freak has won."

Adam nodded. "Atta girl!" His smile softened. "Are you sure? We could turn around right now, and leave the country, and…"

"If I'm running away, I won't be safe," I admitted. "I want to feel safe because I am living my life." I took his hand. "Sorry."

He looked more in love with me then, than he had in five years.

He leant over and kissed my forehead. It made my cheeks burn.

*

The band played old favourites, in a smooth, acoustical style, pared back to make the most of the singer's voice. The caterers did themselves proud with finger food offered on stylish silver trays. The stained glass waterfalls were breath taking, they sealed us in a fantasy world.

For a long while I just lingered on the dance floor, my head on my husband's shoulder, feeling his breath on my neck, and his touch on my bare back.

"I have to go and schmooze," he said. "Shake hands, and tell people how good they are to buy tickets. Do you want to come, or will you be okay?"

"There's a bar," I said, kissing his cheek. "Just don't be long enough for me to miss you."

He slipped away, his fingers lingering on me as long as possible. I watched him go, and tried to slither off the dancefloor.

Somebody bumped into me. Something jabbed my back.

I span around, but couldn't see who stabbed me. "Adam!"

My head turned weightless. A wave of sleepy,

cosy, warmth flushed through my body. I blinked-
and the world went fuzzy. *The music became
pounding and modern. The stained glass was replaced
by yellow bricks, exposed metal, and a forest of
hanging bulbs.* **I shook my head clear. "Adam!" I
screamed.**

**He turned and tried to push his way back
through the crowd**. *Were they high society types in
dinner jackets and formal dresses, or were they
hipsters dressed to party?*

**I shoved my way past the dancers, running for
my husband**, *and stopped dead when I saw who I had
almost trampled. Tanner skidded around me, holding
up his hands. "Sorry… Entirely my…" He stopped
talking, and his jaw hung open.*

*I could see recognition dawning behind his eyes.
He spent several long, scared breaths trying to work
out how I could be.*

"Me too," I purred, grabbing him into a hug. He

was warm. He was warm, and soft, and held me exactly as he had that day on the station in the rain. "Hi."

He held me close, our tears mingling together.

Tanner lifted his head, and put his lips to my forehead.

In an instant he was gone.

And so was my world. There were the hipsters, the bare bricks, the fairy bulbs in the ceiling, and… Fred.

She was staring at me, her eyes wide. A glass slipped from her numbed fingers and shattered on the floor.

I stroked my hair, and looked down at my dress. "I know right?" I said, lamely. "This dress makes me look stunning?"

"Fuck!" Fred said. "Fuck! How? What? How?"

"I don't know," I said.

"Where did Tanner go?" Fred demanded.

"I don't know!" I held up my hands. "Maybe to my

world? If this isn't my coma dream or something?"

"Can he come back?" Fred grabbed me. "Bring him back!"

"I don't know how he vanished!" I squeaked. "I thought this was a dream!"

Fred glared at me. "Bring my brother back!"

"Cede!" I shouted. "We need to find Cede!"

TANNER'S RIFT

The crowd parted. I thought they were giving me room to stand, but they were making room for a hefty gent with a well-trimmed beard shoving his way through them in a hurry. He screeched to a halt, and stared at me.

He was older and heavier, but I couldn't fail to recognise him.

Adam glared at me. "Tanner!"

"Adam?" I jumped to my feet and grabbed him in a hug. "Oh my God! Adam! You're alive!" I frowned. "Or I hit my head really hard. Are you Adam?"

"Get off me," he snapped. "I'm alive? You are the one who died!"

"It is you!" I shook his hand. "I don't know how this is even remotely possible, but... you were dead," I said softly. "You were both dead. I just saw Callie! She's alive too? And..." I groaned softly. "This is the drug isn't it? Somebody spiked my drink, and..."

"Where did Callie go?" Adam demanded. "How are you here?" He frowned. "Why are you happy to see me?"

It was the last one that confused me. I mean, I wanted to know the answers of the other questions, but that should have been obvious. I nodded, and gave him a sad look. "You were both dead. Now you aren't. Why would I not be happy you are alive, Adam?"

"Do you mean happy I'm alive, or we're alive?"

"Both!" I hugged him.

"I was your enemy, you idiot!" He snapped. "We were fighting each other for Callie!"

I stepped back. "No. You were just somebody who made my best friend happy. I wanted it to be me. It wasn't."

"Oh." He sighed. "I always assumed…"

"Ah." I laughed. "Of course! You didn't get the peace offering. Sorry. I…" I rubbed my head. "I don't know how I'm here, or where Callie went, but she belongs here."

Adam nodded. "Yes. I think I know where to get some answers."

*

We drove through the night, through a London both familiar and alien at the same time. The changes were subtle, but jarring when I noticed them. The meters and electric charging points on every parking space were of a different design. The posters on bus stops were all unfamiliar. Many of the busses were of a model I didn't recognise.

Eventually he parked at a terrace in a remote residential street on the cusp of the city. Adam pointed at the house.

"There we are," he said.

I looked confused. "What's that?"

"My wife's dealer," he muttered.

"Wife?" I smiled, brightly. "Really?"

He nodded.

"Dealer?" I asked, quietly.

He nodded again. "She uses a drug, Drift. It lets her slip into a dream world where she can see… how things might have been. If the dice had come up another way."

"What sort of things?" I asked, my stomach knotting.

"You are going to be on TV," Adam said. "Your sister is married to a lovely woman of Asian heritage. Your inlaws work in the restaurant. You do a video blog. You still have movie night." His knuckles tightened on the wheel. "A little while ago, she thought you felt her, just for a moment. You ran to the beach. It was the first time she understood about your dead father."

I cleared my throat. "My father isn't dead."

"He is, here," Adam said. "She looked him up."

That left me cold and hollow. "How?"

"Do you really want to know?" Adam asked.

I shook my head. "No. Sorry. I..." I straightened. "You think that if the drug made this happen, then her dealer will know how?"

"He's a kook," Adam said, "or a genius. He believes in other worlds, in... stuff like this. He's kind of an expert in the stories of time bubbles and other worlds."

"Okay," I said. "Well, that's more than I know."

We got out the car, and walked to the front gate. Adam looked back at another car as it pulled past. Two men in polo-shirts gave him a look.

"Security," he said.

"Oh," I muttered.

The front door opened. A short man with receding hair, wild behind his ears, ran out, and stared at me through his glasses. He prodded at my jacket, and looked at me. His face broke into a broad grin.

"Hello?" I said. "I think you know a friend of mine! We need help."

"Cede, is it?" Adam asked.

"Ha! It is you!" Cede said, in a richly rolling Scottish accent. "You crossed over!" He stared at me. "Where's California?"

"She was with me, for a second," I said. "Then I was in the same place, but it was different, and…"

"Aha!" Cede said, doing a little dance. "Come in! Come in!"

He ushered us into a living room with a sofa that mostly covered in cats, and walls that were covered in the musings of somebody thinking on a different frequency to me. He rummaged through the notes on the wall, and picked at a cluster of articles torn from newspapers.

"Aha!" He said. "Here we go. There have been tales of people slipping between worlds for centuries, but reliable cases go back to the early fifties. Now, yours is somewhat unique, but if you are anything like the people who found themselves in ghost towns, or towns overgrown with weed and ruin, you will be pulled back to your own world in a few hours."

"How..." I looked at my hands. "How did this happen? Is this because my drink was spiked?"

"Perhaps," Cede muttered. "Or at least, perhaps that was the key, but... May I ask you a personal question?"

I nodded.

"She said you saw her," Cede muttered. "When she... died in your world?"

"I was run over," I said. "I was dying. In

the…confusion, I saw… Callie, floating, drowning. I think maybe I overheard people while I was out of it, and my subconscious tried to make sense of it."

"And," Cede said, "were you aware that after nearly drowning, Callie saw you?"

"What?" I asked.

Cede nodded. "She said it was your ghost. You each saw the other die."

"The cost of our survival," I asked.

"No!" Cede laughed. "A link! You had a bond. Two people of psychic potential met and formed a bond. A closeness. When it was severed perhaps the frayed ends reached out, between worlds, and found a new connection. Perhaps the Drift just gave you both enough of a nudge to draw each other across the veil."

Adam tapped his lips. "So, what happens now?"

"It can not be permanent," Cede admitted.

"People glimpse between the worlds, but within hours they are always snapped back. Give or take a few lingering influences, a stray memory, or two. In time you will each return to your own sides. You just have to wait."

"How long?" Adam asked.

"Twelve hours?" Cede shrugged. "Maybe a few days."

"And..." I looked at my hands. "What am I meant to do until then?"

Cede puffed out his cheeks. "I don't know."

"Help me," Adam said.

I looked at him.

"My wife..." He spoke gently. "My wife mourned her friend for eight long years, so much she turned to this drug to glimpse you, to watch you. I got jealous. I got angry. We... grew more distant than I cared to admit. Help me offer her a gesture. Help me set things right. Please." He took my arm. "Please help me make her happy."

I drew a long slow breath. "Of course. Anything."

He smiled. "Show me how to make her a grilled cheese sandwich?"

I laughed and nodded. I turned around.

There were more pictures on the wall. Photofits and sketches.

"Why," I said quietly, "do you have pictures of my Dad?"

"I don't," Cede snarled. "That is the man who has been snooping around here, rummaging in my rubbish, looking for… something."

"He attacked California," Adam said. "He tried to inject her."

"Ah!" Cede clicked his fingers. "Ah! He did, did he?" He nodded. "Yes! Both ends of the connection get a boost, and… that would do it!"

"Why?" I asked. It hit me suddenly. "Did he do

this to get rid of me from my world?"

"Maybe," Cede said. "I think you are missing a bigger question."

"He's dead on this world," Adam said.

I looked at him. "Then… how is he here?"

"I assume," Cede said, "the same way you are here."

Callie Through The Looking Glass

Cede was… wrong. He was too well kempt, his purple roll neck and tweed jacket were almost smart. His hair was clipped short, and his wireframe glasses were stylish.

He listened to our story in a neat and tidy room, devoid of cats, or notes, painted in neutral colours, with a few chairs, and a zen sand garden. He steepled his fingers.

"With respect," Fred said, testily, "you don't seem surprised."

"No." Beta-Cede said, with a smile. "I am rarely wrong. My experiment may have been a failure, at the university, but it would seem I simply chose the wrong drugs. Enough of a psychic stimulation would have been more successful. I used a tailored LSD variant to open the mind. I should have used Drift."

"Then, what happened?" I asked.

"Somebody perfected my method," Cede said. "He stabbed you with the stimulant, and he boosted your psychic potential. If one or more of you had a natural talent…" He stopped and laughed. "Oh… I bet I know who. Wait here." He marched out of the room, and I got a glimpse of him rummaging in a safe in his office, for a file. "There was one test subject I should never have wasted so much time on. A criminal in prison. He had a fierce potential, but was utterly unreliable he was…"

"Dad!" Fred said, pointing at the photograph in the file. "That is my Dad!"

Beta-Cede shrugged, nonplussed. "That would explain why he chose his targets. He knew of a… link between the pair. If he assumed his son inherited his potential, and if he heard about your visions, he might have thought this experiment was worthwhile."

"But…" Callie frowned. "He attacked me. In my world."

Cede screwed up his face. "Sorry. No. That makes no sense. He would have had to…"

"Yeah," Callie whispered. "He was in my world. He knew what he was doing. He even told me it was to ruin his son's life."

"That's Dad," Fred whispered. "After everything, he always blamed Tanner."

"But…" I rubbed the top of my nose. "How is this ruining his life? I'm alive. He saw me. And you can tell him stuff for me, like… I don't blame him, and I love him, and he was a great friend, and…" I sighed. "And I miss him."

Fred hugged me. "Maybe Dad wants to torture him with being so close, but so far. Perhaps Dad only wanted you to appear, to tell him 'I'm here but can never be yours', or something. Dad was an arsehole. He thought kicking the shit out of Tanner would make him less gay. I don't mind never knowing what he thought he was doing."

"So…" I looked at Cede. "What do we do?"

"Wait," Cede said. "Reality has a pull, a gravity. You can visit others, but you will phase back when the pull becomes stronger than your willpower."

I felt a wave of relief. "And it's safe? I will go home and Tanner comes back here?"

Cede nodded. "Yes."

My heart sank. "Will this happen any time I reach out? We swap?"

"I don't know," Cede said. "This is… new territory, and I was politely asked to leave my studies several years ago now. I am somewhat out the loop."

*

We drank coffee in a place I knew near the museum. It was just me and Fred, nursing lattes, watching the night through a steamed-up window.

"Eight years," Fred said. "Where do we begin?"

"I've been… watching," I said.

"Yeah." Fred looked at me. "I wanted to ask. What

have you been spying on?"

"Movie night, mostly," I said. "Sometimes just life in the kitchen, stuff I miss."

"You know he blames himself?" Fred asked. "Like God flipped a coin for your both and let the wrong one live."

"I know." I shuddered. "If it wasn't for Adam…"

"Yeah," Fred agreed. "A few billion must help."

"It doesn't." I let a few of misgivings I had been burying for far too long, bubble to the surface. "My husband helps, when he's with me. He really did come back into my life a better man, but… we spent a long time bouncing around trying to outrun our troubles, and it just made things worse. When we are together, it's perfect, but a lot of the time we aren't. He strays off on his projects, and… In my world, we all let each other drift apart. I lost track of you, and you never liked me turning up with Adam, and…" I cocked my head. "For years now, when he has gone, being alone with

unlimited cash, is boring. It can only buy stuff. Not friends. Not companionship. Not… movie night." I laughed. "It buys Drift, and Drift lets me escape the apartment, or the galas, or a yacht in Venice where I don't know anybody. It lets me see friends. It lets me see who Tanner would have been. Who he is."

Fred took my hands, and caressed them. "You married him?"

I flushed. "I did. A little do, back home in the US. My family were there, and…"

Fred smiled. "I wasn't?"

"You have your job in Edinburgh. I asked, and I think you tried, but…"

"Edinburgh?" She asked, her eyes lighting up.

I nodded. "It's a nice place."

Her lips curled. "You don't see happy."

"I am," I assured her. "There's just… a lot of grey. I'm not unhappy, or happy, just…"

Fred gave me a serious look. "Okay. How do I

help?"

That question warmed my heart.

Fred pushed her phone across the table. "Okay. Here you go."

I looked at her. "What?"

"You wanted to set the record straight, and make the world right," Fred said. "Tell him. Record it. I'll see he gets it. Tell him everything."

I rested the phone against the wall, lined myself in the shot, hit record, and started talking.

*

We booked a hotel room in a chain hotel a block from my apartment.

I lay on the bed, Fred curled around me, hugging me, watching the tower from the window.

"If you wake up tomorrow," Fred said, "and I'm gone, you can just… go try your key. If you're here, you can come hang at the coast for as long as it takes."

"He's okay," I said. "Adam will look after him."

Fred squeezed me as an answer.

"Your Dad isn't the only thing I checked," I admitted.

"Oh?" Fred asked.

"I tried to look you up, on Social Stream," I said, with a smile. "I offered a friend request, but it wasn't accepted. I don't blame her. We haven't talked in a long time. I saw some of her photographs though. She's married too."

"To some nice Scottish lady?" Fred asked.

I flushed at the thought. "No. Li had to go to Edinburgh for business. She ate out, alone. She asked questions. The Chef came out to talk to her, and there were…sparks. They talked more. Dated…"

Fred's breath was a soft sigh. "We found each other?"

"I think…" I smiled. "I think some people are meant to be. Some people are meant to find each other, in any world, in any history."

"Then you will find a way home," Fred promised. "And... don't give up so easily on your Fred. We are a stubborn breed. Sometimes we need a swift whack from the reality stick."

Rain began to patter against the window.

We watched it until we slept.

When I woke, I was alone. My phone beeped, with a backlog of messages. I called Adam.

"Hey," he said when he answered. "Where are you? Are you okay? Did you..."

"I'm a few streets from home," I said. "Tanner?"

Adam paused. "Hang on." A door open and closed on the end of the line. "Tanner?" He drew a breath. "Gone."

"Okay. Are you at the apartment?"

"Yes."

I felt relief flood my heart. "I will be there soon."

"Are you hurt?" Adam asked.

"No. I was injected with something. Drift, I think. I'm okay."

Adam's voice softened. "We should get that checked out. I'll call some doctors."

"Okay." I said, quietly.

"Is…" Adam drew a breath. "Is it over?"

"Yeah." The words didn't hurt me as I expected. They felt like a weight being lifted from my spine. "I think it is. I think I made it right. It's… what I promised I was going to do, right?"

"Okay." Adam paused a fraction. "We should go home. To your family. Get away from Drift, and scary bald men, and everything for a while?"

"Yes." I agreed without hesitation. "Sure."

TANNER OUTVOTED

Adam refused to stop making grilled cheese until he had perfected the art. His security staff got bored of the stuff. Eventually he gave in, took a break, and ate a few. While we worked, we bounced a few other ideas around.

"It's like…" He shrugged. "I stopped asking her along to my investments, because I tool her all around the world, and we never found a single place that made her happy."

"Maybe," I said, "because you are taking anywhere but the places she was happy. I think she was happy in Kent, and I know she was happy growing up. How often do you go back to her family?"

"They come out and see us a lot," he said. "Wherever."

"Do you go to see them?"

He paused, and looked at his feet. "I never even asked to visit them. I invited them everywhere. I was generous. I could show them…anywhere."

I looked at him. "I would take her home."

"And do what?" Adam smiled. "With money being no object."

"Did she ever make you watch that film about the teenage warlock, on the beach…"

Adam laughed. "Oh. Yes." His laugh dried up. "She always wanted a date like the one in the movie. Turning that barn into a drive in, with a projector, and old horror films… I promised to do it one day, but something always came up. Always."

"Just do it," I said. "I could never afford a film print to do it right. If we were in my world, I could lend you a projector…"

"That would be her Action Dan Annual," he agreed. "I… should have thought of that."

"And buy her fish and chips. It was always her favourite movie night snack."

He put a hand on my shoulder. "By the way, the Action Dan thing was cool."

I paused. "I didn't think..."

He smiled. "A lot happened. I knew about it, I just never really thought about it. You were the jealous loser, and then you were dead. It didn't matter much."

"Tell me she was right about you," I said, evenly. "That this time there were no other women, none of the... messes?" I rubbed the back of my neck. "I'm sorry, that wasn't an accusation. I just want to know she's..."

"No other women," Adam said. "I drink less. I lie less. We tried Drift because it was legal, and wasn't meant to be addictive. I got clean. I knew she used, but never thought it was a problem."

I could have hugged him.

Adam paused. His tone changed a little. "I love her."

I spent the night on Adam's sofa, staring at the ceiling, wondering why it felt like Adam hadn't quite believed those last few words.

I woke in a different sofa on the same spot. The couch in the reception of an office. I slipped away before anybody could notice, hoping I wasn't setting off a burglar alarm or anything.

As soon as I was in the foyer of the building, I rang Fred.

"Hey," I said. "I know I vanished last night, but…"

"I know!" Fred laughed. "You vanished, and Callie was here. Now she's gone, and you are back."

"I want to go home," I whispered.

*

I sat at home, on my sofa, watching the video on my phone for the tenth time in a row.

Callie stared out the screen at me, holding a cup of

coffee, wearing a nervous smile and rosy cheeks. She stared into the camera, and chewed her lips. "I don't blame you. In this life I'm gone and you're here. I know your Callie, Beta-Callie, wouldn't have blamed you, because… when I was her it never occurred to me blame anybody. I'm not going to lie, there have been times these last eight years I wished you were still with me. There are times I needed you, that I needed your strength. You always seemed to think you were weak, or useless, because you won't fight, because you won't throw a punch. Any asshole can fight like that. Not everybody has the strength to love instead. To forgive. To hope."

She paused and seemed to centre herself.

"I Drift sometimes. My life is good, and Adam loves me. He isn't always as good as that as I hoped, but he always tries. He made up for a lot of wasted time, growing up, and doing right by people. He cares for me, so much, but… I get lonely. I spend too much time alone, even when I'm surrounded by people. We call them our friends, but they just move in the same circles as us. I don't have many real friends any more, not like you guys were to me. So, I drift, and I always find you. I always find you, and can pretend for a little while I'm still… part of your life. It means so much to know that I'm still loved and remembered. It's probably creeping you out to hear this, but, it means a lot to even have the illusion of being part of Movie night, because… I can't even talk to you, but then, when we were friends, before we tried to be more, we never really needed to talk."

She brushed tears from her cheeks.

"Message more women on that app. Be yourself. Be kind, and sweet, and do what's right. You will find somebody, and I promise, you will be happy. Little things, little moments of kindness, will always find you love. Don't worry. I'm going to intrude on you less. When I thought it was a dream, an illusion, it was easy. Knowing it's real, that I've been… seeing sides of you that maybe you don't want me to know about, is… not something I can live with too easy, but… it makes it harder to give up. Knowing I can talk to you, that maybe you see me too? I..." She broke into nervous giggles. "I would appreciate it if you saved me a space at Movie night. Just in case either of us is feeling alone?"

I tapped it off.

Fred and Li stepped through from the kitchen, with the coffee pot and fresh pastries.

They flanked me, one sitting either side of me.

Li patted my arm. "Is it me, or doe she seem a lot more like somebody trying to be happy, than somebody who is happy."

Fred toyed with her hair. "That is everything she left for you, but it isn't everything she said. I don't think things are going well with Adam."

"They'll get better," I said. "Adam's working on that. He genuinely wanted my help with that."

Li and Fred looked at each other.

Fred smiled. "And you really helped him?"

"We talked," I said. "I had some ideas."

Li curled against me. "See. There you go proving her right about you."

Fred frowned. "I don't know. Something doesn't add up."

I shrugged. "We just heard different sides of it, from different people."

Fred looked at me. "I meant Dad. What Callie said about Dad trying to… hurt her."

I shuddered with the cold. "I don't like that either, but I don't know what to do about it."

"I do," Fred said. Her body tensed. "You don't have to come with me."

I looked at her. "You want to what… go ask him?"

"Why not?" Fred demanded.

"He could hurt you," I said simply.

"No." Li shook her head. "He could pick a fight he's going to lose."

"Nobody is fighting anybody," I said.

"Outvoted!" The girls snapped together.

Dad's place was a poky little flat on the seventh floor of one of the dense concrete high-rise estates that post-war Britain thought the future was going to look like. The resident's association had clearly been making an effort to keep the litter and graffiti under control, but there was miasma of tiredness and wear that the fresh paint couldn't cover.

Fred and Li marched ahead of me, down the balcony walkway, and hammered on the peeling paint of the front door.

My heart turned to coal, as a shadow moved behind the frosted glass.

Dad stepped out, smiling at us. It was a nasty little smile. He stepped out of his flat, and pulled the door closed behind him. He looked at me. "California recognised me, didn't she?"

"You attacked her," I said.

He smiled. "A means to an end. I did not think she

would have known me. I didn't think you would have broken out the family album."

"How…" I struggled to speak over my racing heart. "How did you do this?"

"Practise." He held up his hands. "There wasn't much else to do, when I was left to rot in prison. One day a whole bunch of us sat some tests, for a professor, and he let me play at experiments for a while. He thought there was something special about me. He drugged me, and talked about my dreams, got me to focus on people, on things. When he was shut down, I still had a good few years to waste, and he gave me a way to be free. Over the years, I was pretty good at it. Then one day, I come home from work, and I find myself on a couch. Another me. One from a world I had been Drifting to for months. He'd worked out how to crack open his head and do more than observe, but… the stupid fecker used LSD. I guess Drift hadn't taken off where you were. Well… I could put that right. I came here, to take a look. When I got home, the Police had been in. A nosey neighbour had seen the dead fuck on my sofa, and…" He whistled. "It suited me to slip away. I could always come here. The more I did it… the more I began to belong here."

I stared at him. "And… what… you experimented with Callie?"

He smiled. "No. I gave her what she wanted."

Li scowl. "By attacking her, and screaming at her you were going to…"

"Destroy my son." Dad nodded. "That's the difference between me and the dead fuck. We both took our revenge. We both ran you down. He bottled it and drove away. I hit reverse and made sure." He touched his heart. "It didn't put anything right. It didn't make prison hurt less. It didn't make tomorrow brighter. He saw another world as a chance at redemption. I see it as a chance to do things right."

Fred tensed up, her fingers curling. "What have you done?"

Dad laughed. "I sent you… her finger in the mail. I showed you proof of life. I showed you what you could have won, the star prize, and now I'm destroying it." He smiled. "I'm the only Drift dealer this side of the divide. I'm the only source of the drug. In a few days I'm retiring. I'm slipping away to enjoy my hard earned cash. I'm closing the door. You can't reach her any more. And you can't save her from what is coming."

"What is coming," I said, "is her husband putting things right for her."

"Oh, please," Dad scoffed. "Why can you see the best in that arrogant little rich boy, and not in me?" He laughed. "He isn't going to save her. He's going to own her."

I shook my head.

"Do you really think those guards were there to protect her from me?" Dad demanded. "Or to keep her where he could watch her?"

Fred was scarlet with rage. "You were working with Adam?"

"I showed him," Dad said, "that his little wife was on too loose a leash. That she needed to be called to heel. That she was thirsty for you."

"But, she isn't," I said. "Dear God, what have you done."

"He doesn't have to believe she is," Dad said, in little more than a whisper. "He only has to believe he might not be able to trust her. After all, what would he have done? What had he done, so many times in the past? I showed him how to be sure she can't reach you."

"What," I whispered, "have you done?"

CALLIE'S HOMECOMING

I sank a little deeper into the luxurious leather seats of the private jet, for when first class didn't offer enough luxury, and watched the clouds skim by.

Adam touched my arm. "Are you going to see him again?"

I glanced aside. "I don't know. I mean... I can't do... whatever happened again. If I did, it could only be by Drifting, and I don't know if I want to see it any more. I made my peace. I set it right."

"But you might?" Adam said.

I hugged him. "I don't want to hide in a dream any more. I want to feel close to people again."

"And you can let him go?" Adam asked.

That was not an easy question to answer. I gave him a helpless look.

"We'll work it out," he said.

"Adam," I said, quietly. "What about the bald guy who stabbed me. Tanner's dad got through our security twice, and I didn't even see him on the dance floor…"

"He won't be a problem," Adam said. "We'll keep out of his reach, I promise."

He gave me one of the looks that I had always loved. I don't know if he had the first clue how to keep that promise, but I knew he would move the stars to make it happen if he needed to. My husband did not give up easily when that look was in his eyes.

He lay a blanket over us both, and for the first time in a long time, I felt safe.

*

My parent's farm had not changed in the three or four years since I had last been here. We parked by the barn, and walked up to the stoop. Mom grabbed me in a hug, squeezing me close, clinging to me. Dad put an arm around us both, and kissed my cheek. We sat on the stoop all evening, eating, drinking, laughing, and being a family.

My room had been redecorated into a guest room, in pastel shades and stained wood. It looked a better, without all my junk, and with a few throw pillows and scented candles. I snuck up on Adam while he was washing, stripped of his shirt and wearing only his pyjama bottoms. I slipped my arms around him, and nibbled his neck with a flurry of kisses.

He smiled at me in the mirror. "It's been a long time since you did that."

"It's been a long time," I said softly, "since you worshipped by titties with kisses, too."

His smile grew. I don't know why the most childish of words, in a soft breathy voice, sent his pulse racing to his trousers, but it was a weapon I was all for using. I reached around and slid a hand down his pants, feeling his excitement, and teasing it.

"They miss you," I said, softly. "All of me misses your kisses."

He turned and followed me into the bedroom, leaning over me, as I freed myself from my clothes. His lips brushed lightly over me, from my neck to my breasts, their touch sending lightning bolts of excitement to my core, and leaving trails of goosepimples behind. He savoured my breasts, lingering on them for long blissful minutes, until I begged him to move on.

He was reluctant, so I rolled him over, pinned him down, and wrapped my legs over him. He closed his eyes, and offered me everything, his body and soul.

We made love slowly, gently, and tenderly, milking every second of the sensation, holding onto the glow of our connection as long as we could, until the levees broke, and we were washed away by the moment.

There weren't any words as we lay together, sweaty, exhausted, pink and giggly. There didn't need to be words, just the warmth of our bodies, and the knotted tangle of our limbs.

*

I was woken by the cool air that filled the space where Adam had been, as he rose from the bed.

"Adam?" I whispered.

"Hey." He kissed my forehead. "Go back to sleep. I have a thing. It's for you."

"Oh?" I asked.

He smiled. "Yeah. Just… whatever you see happening today. Don't ask. Tonight it will all become clear."

I didn't ask.

That didn't stop me wondering. I sat on the stoop with Mom and Dad, drinking ice tea, watching first a trio of classic cars, all chrome and fins, being delivered and scattered around the barn. Then a large screen on a frame, that Dad had to help him assemble, and lastly an old cinema projector and some reels of film.

He came running up the steps to the house, and grabbed my mom. "Hey, sorry, I forgot, please don't cook tonight, I'm making some food, but I kind of need some groceries first. Can you come help me get some shopping?"

Dad looked at me. "You've been getting high?"

I wished he wasn't staring at me like he could see my soul. "It's not like that. Not exactly. I found a drug that…let me see Tanner again."

Dad's expression opened with pain. "The landlord who tried to get you to go out with him?"

"The landlord I asked out," I said. "The

landlord who was there for me. Who made me part of his family. The friend I still miss."

"And you…" Dad waved his hands in a helpless gesture. "You dope yourself to dream of him?"

"If you could dream of a world where Nanna was still alive," I said, "where you could see her getting on with life, still cooking clams in seawater on Saturday night, would you?"

He put a hand on my shoulder. "And you have… troubles from your habit?"

"I did." I hugged him. "I lost track of reality and came close to losing control. Adam kept me tethered, and we're making it right."

Dad stared at me. "Because the way Adam talked about it, you were lost in that dream world, with your ghosts for a while. You lost track of what was real?"

"It was real," I said quietly.

Dad looked so pained.

"To me," I added, quickly.

He understood that and patted my hand. "If you need help holding onto reality, your Man and I will always be here." He chewed his lip. "I know a rehab place you could… treat this."

I kissed his cheek. "I'm home now. With you, and with Adam. I'm not going anywhere."

*

When Adam got home he set to work making grilled cheese, and fries, in the kitchen.

"For the movie," he said.

I laughed. "Not fish and chips?"

"No…" He pointed at the array of pans. "I think you will like this."

Mom and Dad watched us from the doorway, impressed by his enthusiasm.

I stared at the carton of cream, and the different cheeses on the counter. "We're having movie night, in cars, like a drive-in?”

He nodded.

“And…” I pointed at the ingredients. “Your making me a grilled cheese with a French croque sauce, and three different cheeses?”

He smiled.

I grinned. “And does the film include teenagers on a beach?”

“It might,” he admitted.

“You’re making Tanner’s grilled cheese?” I whispered. “You talked to him about all this, didn’t you?”

“No, honey,” Adam said, with what I would have believed was eternal patience. “He’s dead.”

“Okay.” I lowered my voice. “I know a lot of the last few days is hard to believe, but…”

He cupped my cheek. “Oh, Callie… Callie…”

His face was full of sympathy, but his eyes were burning for a break up. They were burning like they had when he walked into an argument, swinging for the takedown, back in the day.

"Yeah. Sorry." I waved a hand. "You know I got confused. Let's not talk about this. Let's have movies, and grilled cheese, and…"

"It was his recipe," Adam said, firmly. "He told me it eight years ago, when he stood aside and gave you his blessing to be happy with somebody else. He was a good man, but everything you saw of him since, was a dream, just a dream."

Mom stepped forwards. "He told us about your ghost Callie. I know he humoured you, and… I don't know if I agree with it. Hopefully the treatment will help soon."

"Treatment?" I asked.

He nodded. "It's why we're here, Callie. You remember? We're going to take you to hospital, in a few days, and they are going to remove the damage that Drift did your blame. A couple of zaps of a laser, and those fused synapsis won't let you find your fantasy world any more. You will be home in, reality, in my world, for good."

My heart turned to flint. "What? Are you crazy? I didn't... I did not agree to this. Mom. I didn't ask for this!"

Adam pulled me into a hug, playing at calming the manic woman. "I know. You get confused. Luckily, before things got too bad, you left papers with our solicitor, to prove your intentions, in case this happened. I'd say they were watertight."

"Mom?" I looked between my parents. "Dad? You can't let this happen?"

"You're ill," Dad said. "And you lied to me earlier. You were telling the truth, when you said the ghost world was real, but you lied to me, to pretend that wasn't what you meant. I... didn't believe you had fallen that far, but then you lied..."

"No." I backed out the door.

Ross and his mate were waiting, their arms crossed.

"It won't hurt you," Adam promised. "It'll just keep you here."

"Then ask me to give up Drift," I whispered. "Trust me to be faithful."

Adam kissed my cheek. Very softly, so nobody else could hear, he said: "I won't lose you to him, or to anybody. Ever again."

The truth hit me like a sledgehammer. "You planned this. You planned all this so I would know it was Tanner. You…wanted this.."

Adam raised his voice for the audience. "Oh, Callie, listen to yourself. Do you really think a ghost told me how to give my own wife, the love of my life, a gesture? I am trying to be kind. I'm not your enemy."

My parents believed him.

That was what scared me most.

"No. Mom…" I held up my hands. "Adam saw Tanner. He was at the ball. I vanished to see Fred, and Tanner was…"

"I know you believe that," Dad said, gently. "We know that."

The security men ushered me back into the farm house. One of them passed Adam something, and a needle jabbed me in the back.

"You!" I gasped.

"Shh." He whispered. "Sleep. You will feel better soon."

TANNER ON THE CASE

I hate flying.

I spent the flight from Gatwick to San Fran Cisco in a fugue of nervous tension. The hours dragged by. I was too tense to sleep, and my mind was rattling around too quick to focus on anything that might pass the time.

Cede sat in the window seat listening to operas on his phone, and making shopping lists. Fred sat in the aisle seat, staring at a paperback without really reading it.

My sister looked at me. "You know we are probably going to be fired from the TV show? Missing filming is a pretty big deal."

"Bigger than this?" I asked.

"No." She smiled weakly. "I just wanted you to appreciate how much we are throwing at this."

"I can't believe he would do this," I muttered. "It's…"

"Her jealous ex being jealous and doing something

really stupid?" Fred tutted. "I'd believe it. I told you he was a wanker."

"I know," I said. "But, I made it so much easier, didn't I? When I turned up, he must have struggled not to laugh. I gave him the easiest possible way to give Callie all the rope she needs to hang herself. He didn't even have to Drift himself, or pretend I got a message to him. I really did get a message to him. I…did this."

"It isn't your fault," Cede said, without looking up. "Your father has had a lot of practice at bullying and manipulation."

I sighed. "It's my responsibility though."

"If the link is still strong," Cede said, "and if my other self was correct, you will be able to reach her, as long as we can be sure of where she is."

"That," I said, "is the one thing I am certain of."

*

I rented a campervan, (the salesman kept correcting me, to a Recreational Vehicle, but it was a van in which one went camping, so…) as Cede and Fred went shopping. He brought the raw ingredients for a dirty prison-brew version of Drift. She brought everything we needed for a one-pot curry.

I picked them up from the superstore, and we went and got ourselves lost in the wild hills and grassland, somewhere the sheriffs were unlikely to stumble upon us with awkward questions. I parked in a shady nook beneath a tree, and cooked the curry outside, so Cede could use the kitchen in the van for his drug baking.

I tried not to look at the ingredients he was using. He had three carrier bags full of industrial products covered in warning labels. The sounds and smells from the kitchen were pretty toxic. He was wearing a gas mask.

"This is a really bad idea," Fred said, browning the chicken thighs.

"I know," I said, chopping the onion, chili, garlic, and ginger. "What other choice do I have? The procedure is risky. It is so incredibly risky, and he is doing it for a chance it might stop her using a drug again, that…" I drew a breath.

"She would give me up for him. You know that right?"

Fred nodded. "Does it strike you that's the wrong way around?"

"In an ideal world," I said. "That isn't the hand we got dealt."

"Maybe she has given you up for him," Fred said. "If he loves her like I love Li, with or without my perfect night…"

"Then I get good news, and I walk away," I said, dropping my ingredients onto the chicken. "Nobody that side need ever know." I closed my eyes. "Are you willing to gamble?"

"I held her as she cried," Fred said. "No. I am not willing to take that gamble."

Cede stepped out of van, and lifted off his mask. He sniffed the air. "That," he declared, "smells really nice."

"Good!" Fred beamed. "How are you doing."

"I just need a quiet word with Tanner." Cede waved me over. "Tanner, listen…"

He jabbed a syringe in my arm, and pumped something that felt like battery acid into my veins. It made my heart thunder.

"There," he said. "By the time we reach the farm, that will be kicking in, and I will give you stage two."

"Stage two?" I spluttered.

"Unlike your father," Cede snapped, "I care if you reach the far side veil with your brains intact. Stage two has to be after a full stomach, so…"

I nodded.

*

I got my second (worryingly anti-freeze blue) shot as we reached the edge of the orchards around the farm. Callie took over the driving, and pulled up by the barn. Ma and Pa Gregory came walking out onto their porch, with an amiable but cautious manner.

The world blurred.

"Mom! Please!" Callie begged somewhere inside the house.

I stumbled from the van, with my hands held up. "I am sorry. I know this is out of the blue, and I don't want to try and…"

I trailed off. There was a small convoy pulling up outside the house, with a private ambulance in the middle. Adam met the orderlies with a smile.

"You have to help her," he insisted, "she is losing herself, and I am really scared."

"And?" Pa Gregory asked.

"I'm sorry," I said. "Callie needs me."

"What?" He demanded.

I didn't stop to listen. I ran past him and into the house. "Callie! Where are you?"

She didn't hear me, but there was shouting from the top of the stairs.

Ma Gregory was crying in the sitting room. She stared at me, confused. "Who are you?"

"Is Callie alive or dead here?" I asked.

She stared at me.

"Sorry," I said. "I'll show myself up!"

Adam saw me, from the porch. His face turned to a masque of fury. "Stop him!"

I ran up the stairs. Pa Gregory was hurrying after me. He had a shotgun, that he was hurrying to load.

"Stop!" He barked. "I don't want to hurt you, but I will if you think you can rob from me!"

"Callie!" I shouted.

"Tanner?" She hammered on the door to a bedroom.

I threw open the door. Beyond was a room preserved like a shrine. Shelves stuffed with books, and mementos, walls covered in posters, and charts about Egyptian history.

"My daughter," Pa Gregory said, kindly, but down the barrel of a shotgun, "is dead. Don't go doing whatever this is. Please."

"I'm sorry," I said, pulling the door closed.

It shook, under the hammering blows of desperate fists. **"Tanner! How are you here?"**

I leant against the door. "Hold on. I'm going to try and pull you across to me. Okay?"

"Is..." Pa Gregory lowered his gun. "Is this a joke?"

"I hope not," I said, **clinging to the pull of the other reality as hard as I could. I crouched by the door, and looked through the keyhole. Callie was in her pyjamas, in an emptier room with more modern colours.**

A gun barked. A bullet tore at the doorframe.

Adam levelled his pistol at me, a long barrelled target pistol. "Step away from her Tanner."

Pa Gregory leapt away from the fresh bullet hole in the doorframe. "What was that?"

"Sorry," I said again. **"Callie?"**

I threw myself at the door. It smashed open under my weight, the lock giving way. Callie caught me as we fell together to the floor. I lay over her, my cheek beside hers.

Adam stepped in the doorway, and pressing the warm maw of his pistol to the back of my head.

"Don't!" Callie screamed. "Please. I'll…"

"Enough," Adam snarled. He breathed heavy, trying to force himself to pull the trigger. "That's enough. You are dead, right? I can't murder a dead man."

"Don't," Callie begged, in tears.

Ma Gregory, the one from Callie's world pumped a round into a shotgun, and pointed it at Adam, her eyes like flint. "Now. I think we all need to hang on a moment, and you need to tell me what's going on."

My grip on the world shook. I could feel myself being pulled home. Callie looked me in the eye, and wrapped her fingers around mine.

"Mum," she whispered. "I might be gone a day or two. If I don't come home, it was real, and I am going where my asshole of a husband can't lay a finger on me. Okay?"

Ma nodded.

Callie squeezed my hand, closed her eyes and kissed me.

"What the Hell?" Pa Gregory asked, behind me.

Callie gasped, and laughed. She sat up, looking at the toys, and the posters. Her eyes fell on her Dad. She smiled weakly. "Hey."

He dropped to his knees. Ma Gregory came sprinting up the stairs, and crashed to a stop. For a moment we were all frozen, then with a squeal of delight, and floods of tears, Callie tore herself from me and wrapped her parents in an embrace.

"How?" Ma asked.

"What?" Pa asked, clinging to her. "I love you. I love you. I…"

Callie sobbed. "It is a long story. Just promise me you'll believe it? And if Adam turns up, point a fucking gun at him?"

"I'm sorry," I said, rubbing my head. "I… would have warned you, if…"

They weren't listening. I stepped around them.

"Tanner?" Callie said.

"Take your time," I said. "I'll be outside when you need me."

She held my gaze for a long time. "How long do I have?"

I gave her a helpless shrug. "I don't know. Maybe we shouldn't be here when you go back."

Callie smiled. "I don't think I will be going back."

"To Heaven?" Ma asked.

Callie looked at me. "No. Not even close. If Tanner makes me something to eat, I will tell you all about it."

CALLIE'S EVERAFTER

It took either of us a long time to believe I was here for keeps. We spent the first few weeks living like I might vanish at any moment. Somebody had to prise me away from Tanner before he could go on camera. The guys at the restaurant thought it was sickening.

Then, on the run up to Christmas, I was hanging out at the restaurant, when Li started squeaking, and dragged me front of house. My Cede, and their Cede were having dinner together. My Cede, the one with the cats, was upset that "the whole of causality might have been misaligned or something".

"What's wrong?" I asked, as Tanner slipped his arms around me.

"He," Cede said, "didn't pull on your link. He tied it in a knot."

"You," the other, colder Cede said, "are stuck

here."

I smiled. "I know."

Tanner didn't say anything. His hold on me said it all.

"It explains a lot," I admitted.

I should be honest. I didn't come with Tanner intending to be stolen into a relationship, but to be fair, he had saved my life, and our adrenaline had been thumping through our veins, and I needed to believe I was safe, so… I didn't mourn my marriage all that long. Or at all.

We tried to pretend that it wasn't happening. He told me straight up, that he didn't want to be the guy who took advantage of me, which made me want it more. Then things just… happened. One night I crossed the hall from his spare room to his, put a finger on his lips, and let him entwine me in an embrace.

Once we started, it just… swept us away.

That was when I knew: Me and Fred had been

right that night in the hotel. The right people find a way to be together, no matter what world you happen to live in.

Every day since was a gift. I'm not going to waste any of them.

With Thanks

Grant Leishman

Tracy Robinson

Sally Ann Cole

Deborah Garland

Ann Turton

May J Panayi

Cam Gant